THE UNOFFICIAL

COLLEGE

GUIDE TO

Other Ivy League Murder Mysteries
from SparkCollege:

The Unofficial Guide to Yale . . . with Murder!

THE UNOFFICIAL
COLLEGE
GUIDE TO

HARVARD

WITH MURDER

OR . . . EVERYTHING YOU EVER WANTED TO KNOW
ABOUT HARVARD BUT WERE TOO ~~AFRAID~~ TO ASK.

SPARKCOLLEGE
AN IMPRINT OF SPARK PUBLISHING

WWW.SPARKCOLLEGE.COM

This book has not been endorsed by Harvard University. All descriptions of Harvard and opinions about Harvard are solely the views of the authors. This is a work of fiction. All names, characters, incidents, and dialogue are imaginary, and any resemblance to persons living, deceased, or undead is entirely coincidental.

Written by John Crowther, Josh Cracraft, and Kim Holmes.

SparkCollege is an imprint of SparkNotes LLC

Spark Publishing
A Division of Barnes & Noble
120 Fifth Avenue
New York, NY 10011
www.sparknotes.com

ISBN-13: 978-1-4114-9870-9
ISBN-10: 1-4114-9870-4

Library of Congress Cataloging-in-Publication Data

The unofficial college guide to Harvard—with murder: everything you ever wanted to know about Harvard but were too dead to ask.
     p. cm.
1. Harvard University—Fiction. 2. Cambridge (Mass.)—Fiction. 3. College students—Fiction. 4. College stories.

PS3600.A1U54 2006
813'.6—dc22

                                        2006023876

Please submit changes or report errors to www.sparknotes.com/errors.

Printed and bound in the United States.

1 3 5 7 9 10 8 6 4 2

Acknowledgments

The authors would like to thank:

Lauren Jackson for letting us pick her brain and doing some ground research for us, as well as the crew building the new Harvard Pub. Best of luck!

Rich Lim, Brian Sandoval, Jason Kim, Shinah Chang, and Mindy Wu for brainstorming, reading drafts, and listening to us complain.

Emily Wu, Natalia Mendoza, Michelle Young, Meyeon Park, Kelsey Corlett, and Mauli Shah for their two cents on the houses, frosh dorms, societies, clubs, courses, parties, relationships, and other Harvard miscellany.

Maureen Johnson—you meant more to us than you'll ever know.

Dan Weiss and Robert Riger for inspired leadership and for making this project happen.

And, finally, Laurie Barnett, whose creative vision and passion inspired our efforts from concept to finished book, as they do every day we work with her.

Introduction

What you are about to read is not real . . . well, there's no real murder, anyway.

What *is* real is the information about Harvard. This story is stuffed with need-to-know facts, large and small, about all things **Cantab**. Our crack team of Harvardites have given up their hard-won knowledge and infused it into a murder mystery.

In the story, you'll notice that the bold Harvard-related terms are defined along the sides of the pages. These nuggets of solid gold will tell you all about the ins and outs of choosing classes, picking a **concentration**, feeding yourself, navigating between the Quad and the river, understanding the Final Club system, **renting a Picasso** for your room, surviving the punishing workload, mocking Yale properly, and maybe even finding some sweet Cantab love.

And whether you want to find out more about

Cantabs: Here's your first fact: Harvard students are sometimes called "Cantabs." It's an abbreviation of Cantabrigian, meaning "a person who lives in Cambridge." You did know Harvard is in Cambridge, right?

concentration: Harvardese for "major."

renting a Picasso: This is absolutely real. One of Harvard's main art galleries, the Fogg, is filled with Greek, Roman, medieval, and European masterpieces. Lots o' good stuff here, including some drawings, prints, and paintings that you can rent. And we're not talking Koko the gorilla finger paintings here. For twenty-five dollars you can rent original stuff from modern masters such as Joan Miró and even Picasso.

the school before you apply, or you just want to avoid embarrassing freshman-year mistakes, be sure to check out these vital nuggets of Harvard lore:

One

So it's come to this, Parker Norcross thought wryly.

As the snow piled in drifts on the windowsill of her Harvard dorm room and the wind whistled eerily out in the darkness of a Cambridge winter, Parker stared skeptically at the Styrofoam cup of ramen she held in her hands.

Parker was probably the only person at Harvard—or any college, for that matter—who had never once tried ramen. Well, to be fair, she had never tried packaged ramen. A world traveler who prided herself on her ability to scout out the best meal on whatever continent she happened to be at the time, Parker had more than once eaten fresh ramen at traditional roadside stands in Japan. (And you could always trust her to somehow know the best roadside stands, the ones not even mentioned in the *Let's Go* guidebook.) But that ramen—the steaming hot noodles with thick slabs of sliced pork—looked nothing like the dusty, shrunken shreds she was considering forcing down her throat now.

The Adams House dining hall: Harvardese for "cafeteria." Adams dining hall is one of the most convenient dining halls on campus, which is why admittance is usually restricted to Adams residents and their guests. Elitist pigs!

Intersession: That sweet, sweet week between the end of January finals and the beginning of the second semester. Everyone goes to Europe or the Caribbean.

Porsche: Only the fabulously wealthy can afford to own a car at Harvard. Parking alone will cost you $1,500 a year.

But Parker was in a fix. The Adams House dining hall was closed for Intersession. Going outside to forage was not an option, as the worst blizzard in twenty-five years had just descended on Boston. Outside the window, the wind kept up its eerie whistling, causing snow-covered branches to slap noisily against Parker's window. She frowned, tucked a stray strand of her expensively coifed, ashy blond hair behind her left ear, fiddled nervously with the David Yurman bracelet on her wrist, and peered outside. The courtyard was smothered by mounds of blinding white snow. The entire Cambridge landscape was equally desolate. Parker's fox-trimmed Searle coat was still hanging from the hook on her door, heavy and wet from the snow it had absorbed during the walk home.

Parker's chances of leaving Cambridge were looking slimmer by the second. Her flight to Barbados was cancelled, and the train station was snowed in, so she couldn't even go back to her parents' house on Park Avenue in Manhattan. Her suitemates had all finished finals and departed campus the day before, leaving her completely by herself. To make matters worse, Parker quickly realized that she'd left her electric kettle in her **Porsche**, which meant she would have to wait a few days—or bury herself neck-deep in snow—before she could even eat that cup of ramen.

All the better, she thought. She had managed to find gourmet meals in more unlikely circumstances than this. With a disdainful glance, she tossed the Cup O' Noodles into the trashcan alongside her worthless plane ticket, slipped a hooded "**Yale**" **sweatshirt** over her head, and sauntered out the door. There had to be someone else in the house with food on hand, Parker mused. Something more savory, or at least less mummified, than ramen.

A solution to both of those issues soon presented itself to Parker in the form of Dunston Peck, her next-door neighbor. As Parker peered though the open door to his room, she found Dunston hard at work at his desk, wearing a worn silk brocade dressing gown and slippers. Strange music warbled in the background as Dunston bent carefully over what appeared to be some sort of rack for mounting or displaying objects.

"Dunston?" she asked.

Her neighbor looked up and made a dry clicking sound with his mouth. Putting down the implements he had been holding, he rubbed his hands together nervously and smiled.

"Why my dear Miss Norcross, this is an

Yale sweatshirt: The wearing of anything from Yale is a joke around Cambridge. The Harvard-Yale rivalry is fun and pointless, though the Yalies take it far too seriously. Like the French, Yalies have an ENORMOUS inferiority complex and will take every opportunity to tell anyone who'll listen why Yale is so much better than Harvard. Cantabs'll make a stab or two at Yale until something more interesting distracts them, such as *American Idol* or a leaf fluttering by.

unexpected pleasure."

"It's Parker, Dunston. I've been telling you for the last three years to call me Parker."

"Of course, of course, my dear lady."

Parker sighed. Dunston was the **kind of kid you could only find at Harvard.** At eighteen, he had assisted with ten archaeological digs in Egypt alone, not to mention a few "jaunts" to China and Rome. He had once bragged to Parker that he had read the Heqanakht Papyri on the *original papyrus*, which would have impressed her if she had known what the Heqanakht Papyri were. Even though he knew nothing about science, Dunston would sometimes sneak into the chemistry labs in the **Science Center** because he "liked the preservative smell of formaldehyde." There was even a rumor that Dunston had had a brief romantic entanglement with one of his anthropology professors, which wasn't completely unheard of at Harvard, aside from the fact that the professor in question was seventy-six years old. Most Harvard students would agree that Dunston took his attraction to relics a bit too literally.

Although Harvard provided Dunston with a seemingly unlimited resource of old things, places, and, well, people, he had made his dorm room in A-**entryway** the hub for his intellectual

kind of kid you could only find at Harvard: Let's just get it out of the way. You're going to meet some unusual types at Harvard. You might want to take a second to look at the list of Harvard student types at the end of this chapter. We'll wait.

Science Center: The big butt-ugly building just north of the Yard with large lecture halls and sardine can–size classrooms. The trippy architecture and artwork offset its otherwise bland purpose to house labs, offices, computer rooms, a science library, and the freshman mailroom.

entryway: A group of suites in a frosh dorm arranged around a central stairwell, akin to a vertical hallway. So A-entryway would be a cluster of six or seven suites next to B-entryway, another cluster of six or seven suites.

and personal pursuits. Decorated like a Moroccan pleasure pad from the 1920s, Dunston's
room was swathed with rich velvet drapes and
throw pillows, all in the same dark **crimson**.
Every nook and cranny of the room was cramm-
ed with rare finds from Dunston's archaeological digs, eBay purchases, and antique store
expeditions.

"What's that you're listening to?" Parker
asked.

Dunston made the clicking sound again and
gestured toward an immaculate phonograph in
the corner of the room, next to an old, yellowing
globe.

"My brand new recording of Schubert's *El-
lens dritter Gesang*, or, as the layman calls it, *Ave
Maria*."

"Brand new?" Parker questioned, raising an
eyebrow.

"Why, yes," he replied. "I picked it up along
with a 1923 copy of Billy Murray singing 'Tiddle-
Dee Winks.' Truly a rare haul."

"Wow," she said politely. "Listen, Dunston,
do you have any food?"

"Are you hungry, my dear Miss Norcross?" he
asked. "In a situation like this, snowed in and
unable to . . . *escape*, one is forced to fall back
on whatever happens to be in the fridge at the

crimson: Fair
Harvard's color and
(sadly) mascot. While
other schools are
the "Cougars" or the
"Spartans" or even the
"Fighting Irish," Harvard
is "The Crimson."
Lame, we know.

moment." He bent over to peer into a small refrigerator lurking under a Moroccan drapery. After a moment's reflection, he spoke. "You don't have a problem with organ meats, do you, Miss Norcross?"

Parker thought about the sweetbreads with pancetta and *glace de veau* she had devoured the weekend before at Le Cirque while visiting her parents. She thought about the *pâtés* of coarsely chopped, veiny goose livers she had wolfed down in Switzerland on artisanal bread; the calf brains she had swallowed whole as a young girl, in the days before mad cow disease. An intrepid gourmand, Parker decidedly did *not* have a problem with organ meats or *charcuterie* of any kind.

She might, however, have a slight problem with dormmates who just "happened" to have organs lying around their rooms.

"Not really, no; that might not be so—just what the hell do you have in there anyway, Dunston?"

"Oh, you know, Miss Norcross. Odds and ends, odds and ends. Do sit down, my dear," Dunston said, moving some books off a wicker chair. "Pardon the mess. I receive visitors so infrequently, you know." He picked up a small vial of lotion and began rubbing it on his hands distractedly. "So irritated—always so irritated," he muttered.

"*What* are you irritated about, Dunston—do you want me to leave or something?"

"Oh no, oh no, dear lady. I wouldn't dream of it, wouldn't dream of it! It's my hands that are irritated." He nodded toward the mounting case he'd been working on when she had come in. "*Thaumetopoea processionea*. Oak processionary moths."

"Oh, so you collect butterflies? How, uh, nice, Dunston."

"Moths. And they're not really, my dear. Nice, that is. Deadly to humans, you know. Contact with their larvae causes blistering and inflammation of the skin and . . . membranes." Dunston held up his hands and sighed, then extended the lotion bottle toward her invitingly.

Parker was less and less sure that she wanted Dunston preparing her food, and she certainly didn't want to share his lotion.

"Of course, people didn't always fear processionary moths. The ancient Romans, for example, used to smear them on their genitals to heighten sensitivity during lovemaking."

"Eww, Dunston, that's gross!" Parker said, knocking over a shoebox full of antique daggers as she jumped out of her chair backward toward the door. "Oh, sorry about that. . ."

"Now, let's see what we can do about that snack, my dear."

"Oh, you know . . . " Parker said, backing away slowly. "I was supposed to go . . . somewhere. Like, now. And I totally forgot until just this second."

"In this storm?" Dunston asked.

"Yeah . . . " she said slowly. "I have to go to return something. A book. To a friend."

"Well, well, my dear. Another time, perhaps? Come by any time. I get so few visitors, for some reason."

"Yes, yes!" she said quickly. "Let's do that soon! Thanks so much!"

The escape was a narrow one. But by this point, Parker had had enough. When it was time to eat, it was time to eat, storm or no storm. Without even stopping at her own room to grab her coat, she proceeded directly to the lobby. She pushed her way through the front doors and out the main entrance. She was greeted with a blast of cold, icy air to the face that nearly bowled her over. In that one moment, she had a horrible realization: her **swipe card** was in her wallet. Which was in her coat pocket. She made a desperate lunge for the door, but it shut with a click before she could catch it with her outstretched hand.

She was stuck outside in the middle of the worst storm in modern Cambridge history.

swipe card: Your university photo ID card also serves as your swipe key to enter your dorm or house. It also lets you check out library books, make photocopies, and get food at the dining hall. Without it, you are lost.

Colorful Characters

The 12 Types of Harvard Students

The Legacies

Born with platinum spoons in their mouths, these sons and daughters of prominent politicians and captains of industry come to Harvard merely to carry on the age-old family tradition. Get to know as many of these gentlemen and women of leisure as you can—their croquet games are jolly good fun, and they're the only kids with cars.

The Backwoods Hicks

Sadly, the Freshman Dean's Office feels compelled to admit a few hicks every year to maintain some semblance of "diversity." And to make sure every state is represented. Whether from the badlands of Montana, the cornfields of Kansas, or the bayous of Louisiana, these kids lay low and keep their Red State views to themselves.

The Commies

These die-hard champions of the Bostonian proletariat devote their undergraduate lives to social service and overcoming the stigma of attending an Ivy League institution they know will eventually make them wealthy plutocrats. Find them volunteering at Phillips Brooks House Association or pitching protest tents in the Yard to support the weekly cause.

The Wonder Kids

These freakishly smart whiz kids enter Harvard at an age when the rest of us were still wallflowers at middle school dances. Don't let the bubble gum and hormonal imbalances scare you, though, because their keen intellect will come in handy the night before the organic chemistry final. Not yet legal, but hey, neither are you.

The Techies

Self-proclaimed geeks and freaks such as these nerds hide away in their rooms until dropping out to found tech startups—such as Microsoft, Facebook.com, and SparkNotes—in their moms' garages. Blessed are the meek, for they will inherit the earth.

The Snipers

These intense, brooding college freshmen in their mid-twenties understandably have trouble getting wasted with their underage roomies. Still, most have interesting stories to tell of fighting drug lords in Colombia, meditating with Himalayan monks, or sniping terrorists for the Israeli army. No, really.

The Premeds

Although most entering freshmen harbor pipe dreams of one day attending med school, the serious few mean business. These impersonal, party-pooper premeds flock to the Cabot Science Library during Reading Period and glare icy daggers of death at anyone who disturbs them. Shh! This is a library!

The Demons of the Deep

Pale, pasty, and agoraphobic, these vampires lurk in the shadows of the sub-basement crypts of Widener and Pusey Libraries, only emerging at night for quick bites of pizza (or people?). Don't be surprised to find them peering out at you from behind the stacks or suddenly vanishing when you swore you'd just seen them a second ago. They are there . . . and watching . . .

The Celebs

Everyone says these glitzy glam kids are just normal students, but no one really believes any of that crap. Pop idols, teen heartthrobs, and crown princes are just a few of the fabulously famous you'll meet—and secretly stalk—at Harvard. Happy hunting.

The Jocks

Nope, not even Harvard can avoid jocks, although the majority of students do look down on them in a perverse, yet highly satisfying, twist of fate. Then again, don't immediately dismiss that giant rugby player who's missing his front teeth—he may just be a Fulbright Scholar fluent in Arabic.

The Psychos

According to one study, Harvard has more than its fair share of students incapable of feeling empathy or remorse. Just as likely to set the multivariable calculus curve as gut you like a fish, these psychopaths only look out for number one. Hello, Clarice . . .

The Rhodes Scholars

These multitalented wonders have the grades and the skills that make even Harvard kids jealous. Yet despite their six-class course load in statistics and ancient Babylonian history, their ongoing search for extraterrestrials, and that sketchy experiment involving human embryos, they still seem to have more free time than everyone else. Find them training for the Olympics, playing Hamlet, addressing the Senate, or hanging out with the Andean shepherds of Peru.

TWO

Parker pressed her face against the glass pane of the door and stared inside.

"Okay, no need to panic," she said.

Her hot, ragged breaths fogged up the window. She wiped it with her sleeve and peered inside. The lobby was deserted. As she squinted, the blurred marble faces on the wall-length fireplace looked as though they were mocking her.

Under any other circumstances, she wouldn't have had anything to worry about. She could usually count on someone walking by on the way to the dining hall or the library to let her in. But since it was Intersession and there were fewer than thirty people left in the house, the odds of that happening were significantly slimmer.

Parker slumped down with her back against the door. The snow showed no signs of stopping, and the drifts loomed large, coming up to her shoulders.

I'm going to die, she thought. *I'm going to die a stupid, stupid death. And I'm going to do it in a Yale sweatshirt.*

Suddenly the door swung open, and Parker collapsed in a shivering heap on the lobby floor, banging her elbow painfully on the molding.

"Ow!"

Rubbing her throbbing elbow, Parker looked up into the smirking face of Neesa Barnett, perhaps the one person in Adams House—or the world for that matter—for whom Parker would have preferred to stay outside.

"Parker!" Neesa exclaimed. "What the hell are you doing sitting outside in the worst snowstorm ever to hit Cambridge, like some kind of moron? Exams are rough, but there are smarter, more *efficient* ways of ending your life than freezing yourself to death."

"I forgot my swipe card," Parker mumbled, propping herself up on the ground.

"Well, get up," Neesa said brusquely, grabbing Parker by the elbow and yanking her off the floor. "Have you eaten? I'm going to Quincy to meet Paul and a few friends. You should join us." Neesa had a habit of taking charge of everyone around her, whether they were her friends or not.

"Well . . . "

"Of course you'll join us," said Neesa, very matter-of-factly. "It's a quick walk."

She plucked the fabric of Parker's sweatshirt lightly.

"I like it," she added. "I think it's very bold of you to forgo fashion for irony."

Neesa Barnett was a full head shorter than Parker, but ever since Parker had known her, she had had the uncanny ability to make Parker feel much, much smaller. With her flowing chestnut hair, olive skin, and brown eyes like liquid pools, Neesa had become a campus celebrity ever since she arrived in Cambridge for **Freshman Week**.

But Neesa wasn't only pretty to look at. She was a force to contend with in the classroom too. She could show up to Parker's Samuel Beckett seminar after a solid night of partying at **the Spee**, sit down, and rattle off a brilliant analysis of the dramatic structure of *Footfalls* without missing a beat. She was the darling of the English Department and had always bragged to anyone who would listen that she would **come back for her PhD** after her senior year. With her stellar **GPA** and purportedly brilliant thesis (a tremendous buzz had already been generated, mostly promulgated by Neesa herself), Neesa's dream was soon to become a reality.

Parker's problem with Neesa was

Freshman Week: The week freshmen move in, when upperclassmen are still enjoying the end of their summer break. Lots of meeting and greeting and hanging out with people you'll actively avoid the rest of your four years when you're no longer desperate for friends.

the Spee: One of the many Final Clubs featuring rushes and parties, filled with young Harvard men who still can't get over the fact that they weren't invited to join the elite Porcellian Club. Final Clubs are glorified frats filled with guys way too smart for Delta house but not yet mature enough to drink responsibly.

come back for her PhD: Staying at Harvard to do your graduate work is ridiculously hard. So what if you went there as an undergrad? So what if you've published and spent years researching your entrance essays? The professors who make the choices about whom to admit are, quite frankly, sick of the sight of you.

GPA: While every other school in America calculates GPA on a 4.0 scale, Harvard is not just every other school. Oh no, it's the best, which means it gets not a 5.0 or a 6.0 but a 15.0 scale. Uh-huh, you heard right—15 friggin' points. It actually kinda makes much more sense, though: 15=A, 14=A-, 13=B+, 12=B . . . Ah, yes, and Harvard doesn't give "Fs"; it gives "Es" if you completely bomb. Just one of the many ways Harvard is better.

she could never tell:
College is like that. You
often can't tell whether
you can't understand
your fellow students
because they're smarter
than you or because
they're not making any
sense.

that **she could never tell** whether Neesa was her
mortal enemy or a rather prickly friend, just as
she could never tell whether Neesa was simply
too brilliant for her to understand or a pretentious fraud who simply didn't make any sense
most of the time.

Parker's confusion on both of these points
dated to the first day in their Victorian Lit Expos
course freshman year. To the bewilderment of the
rest of the class—but the enthusiastic approba-
tion of the instructor—Neesa had been busily ex-
pounding her theory of how George Eliot's style
of third person omniscient narration constructed
an authorial subjectivity that was decidedly mas-
culinist and, indeed, phallogocentric, reinforcing
the most patriarchal view of authorship, when
Parker, who was following about every third
word, timidly raised her hand and interjected:

"But wait—George Eliot was actually a
woman, right?"

There was a moment of silence as Neesa and
the instructor regarded her—contemptuously, it
seemed to Parker. Then, with a roll of her eyes
and an "of course, dear," Neesa continued on
as if the interruption had never happened. Had
Parker embarrassed Neesa or merely made a fool
out of herself? Did Neesa want Parker's respect
and admiration, or did she only want to outdo

and undercut Parker at every turn? Parker could never really be sure. And now, as usual, Parker was following Neesa obediently. At least, she told herself, she was going to do what she'd set out to do. There was dinner involved.

The pair waded through snowdrifts across Mount Auburn Street, which—like all of Cambridge, was now deserted of traffic—then into the courtyard of Quincy House. Neesa swiped her card at the entrance and led the way up the stairs to the second floor. Parker thought wistfully of the student-run hamburger grill on the first floor, now closed. Neesa flung open the doors of the dining hall with a flourish and scanned the oak-paneled room like a proud lioness surveying her tribe.

"There's everyone!" Neesa said, pointing to a table.

Parker looked over to see a table of upperclassmen whom she recognized by sight but had never actually met, as all three were usually too involved with their respective clubs to have much time to mingle with outsiders. At the near end of the table was Paul Alexander, a member of the fabled **Porcellian Club**. Like Parker's, Paul's family had a house on Park Avenue in Manhattan. He wore a tweed jacket and a navy rep tie decorated with little gold pigs. He nodded at Parker with a

Porcellian Club: The most elite Final Club. See "Join Up!" on page 111.

sleek, self-satisfied air.

Next to Paul was Ben Roth, an earnest, slender young man who was a senior officer in the **Signet Society**. Gaunt and pale from staying up every night editing the society's **literary quarterly**, he glanced nervously at Parker, pushing his horn-rimmed glasses up on his nose, then looked awkwardly back at his plate. Parker reflected that talking to women was not his strong suit.

At the far end of the table, paying no attention to his companions and scanning the rest of the room as if looking for fresh prey, was Gordon Clark, one of the famous **Krokodiloes**. Gordon was short, rather plump, and extremely ugly—even fascinatingly so. His thick black hair was slicked back and held in place with some sort of oily emollient, and he was elegantly attired in a navy sport coat and a white shirt with an open collar. He had an air of complete confidence, as if he knew he could have any woman in the room. Parker found herself staring at him in spite of herself. Gordon simply winked at her, making her shiver involuntarily, then ignored her and went back to scanning the room, humming softly to himself.

With a nod of greeting to the table, Parker grabbed a plate and made a beeline for the grill. At the very least, she was going to get some

Signet Society: Harvard's undergraduate literary society, chock-full of wannabe novelists like us.

literary quarterly: The Signet's poetry-filled magazine, which no one ever reads.

Krokodiloes: Harvard's best a cappella crooners. See "Join Up!," on page 111.

hot, decent food out of this experience. She approached the grill attendant with a hungry gleam in her eye.

"I'd like a . . . no, make that two cheeseburgers, please," she said.

"Sorry," said the cook. "The grill is closed during Intersession. We're only serving the buffet options over there." He extended a latex-gloved index finger past Parker's head.

Parker craned her neck to look at the table. It was filled with the remnants of last week's meals—**Mumma's chicken, beef fajita fettuccini, fried cusk.** She lingered over the choices, and by the time she got back to the table Neesa was deep into a discussion of her thesis.

Mumma's chicken . . . fried cusk: Actual dishes you can enjoy at various Harvard dining halls!

"So what's this famous thesis on, again?" Parker asked, with as sincere an interest as she could muster.

"It's about *Carmilla*, by Sheridan Le Fanu," said Neesa, eying Parker like she was a dangerous animal. "Do you know it?"

Parker perked up. "I think I read about it in Victorian Lit," she replied animatedly. "It's a lesbian vampire novel, written about twenty years before *Dracula*, right? Some sort of softcore Victorian erotica? That sounds like fun to work on."

At the mention of the word *lesbian*, Paul

straightened his tie uncomfortably, Ben swallowed so hard his Adam's apple nearly smacked his chin, and Gordon shot Parker a salacious glance.

"Actually, that's almost entirely wrong," snapped Neesa. "The lesbian vampire in Le Fanu's corpus of work is not some fantasy object for horny Victorians to drool over. My paper draws on Lacan's theory of the Mirror Stage to demonstrate that Le Fanu uses the image of the female vampire as an ortho-psychic model of lesbian sexuality, constructing a unique form of subjectivity based on the experience of the female middle-class Victorian reader."

"What the hell does all of that mean?" asked Parker, in genuine bewilderment. "Can anybody on the English faculty actually understand your thesis?"

Neesa ignored Parker and turned her attention back to Paul, who wore the smug expression of someone who had no idea what this beautiful woman was talking about but who would soon be making so much money he could buy and sell Lacanian psychoanalysts like so many pork bellies.

Ben Roth was staring at Neesa adoringly, like a puppy desperate for attention. He pushed his glasses up on his nose and cleared his throat nervously. "Um, Neesa? Do you have a title for your thesis?"

"It's called *Bite Me: Le Fanu and the Lesbian Erotic Vampire Tradition*," Neesa said with a smile, which made Ben turn a shade paler.

"Uh, I think we have a first edition of *Carmilla* back at the

Signet library," Ben said eagerly. "Maybe you'd like to come see it sometime, Neesa. I could take you down into the **Crypt** when the candles are all lit, and we could peruse it together. It might help you with your research." He was getting increasingly excited as he talked.

Neesa dismissed him with an arch smile. "That's nice, Ben. My research doesn't really leave me time for all that *Dead Poets' Society* sort of thing. I'm more into the intellectual, theoretical side of literature. The psychoanalytics of vampirism is going to be the next big thing in English studies."

Ben looked down at his plate, crestfallen. Gordon chuckled and clapped him on the shoulder.

Paul spoke up with a haughty look at Ben. "Dear boy, if she wanted first editions, **the Porc** could buy her her own library full of them."

"Don't be vulgar, Paul," scolded Neesa. Parker, for one, felt that she'd had enough of this conversation. She yawned theatrically.

"Oh, just look at the time," she said. "I'm beat. I'm going to head back up to my room."

"It's only seven thirty," said Neesa. "What are you, like, seventy?"

"I pulled an all-nighter last night to study for my **Ec10** final," Parker answered crisply.

Signet library: Loaded with first editions donated by famous Signet alums, such as T.S. Eliot, John Updike, and Robert Frost. Pretty impressive, actually.

Crypt: Under the Signet lies a dank, candle-filled cave known simply as the Crypt. Here members kick back with a few brewskies, read from their extensive library of first editions, and reenact their favorite scenes from *Dead Poets' Society.* O, Captain, my Captain!

the Porc: Slang for *the Porcellian.*

Ec10: Slang for Social Analysis 10, the introductory economics course. Most people at Harvard take it at some point during their undergraduate careers, no matter their concentration. See "The Freshman 15" on page 71.

CHAPTER TWO | 24

"Oh," said Neesa sympathetically. "I started studying *weeks* in advance. But I hear those all-nighters can be pretty rough. By all means, go home and get some rest. Here's my swipe card. Someone else will let me in, I'm sure."

The snow had gotten considerably deeper in the short time Parker had been at dinner. By the time she reached Adams House, she was coated.

"Why didn't I just go to Stanford?" she asked herself, pulling off her Prada boots and knocking off a pile of white powder.

* * * * *

Parker tiptoed past Dunston's door and heard him singing along to an opera that she actually recognized from her classical music **core class**.

Upon entering her room, Parker immediately plopped herself down on her bed and buried her face in her pillow. What had she done to deserve this? Why was she stuck in Adams House with a group of the weirdest, most antisocial people imaginable?

Barbados. She could be on her way to Barbados.

Parker felt a lump welling up in her throat that began to compete with the lump she felt in her stomach. She reached underneath her bed

core class: The core is the liberal arts component of the curriculum that includes courses on literature, art, science, quantitative reasoning, foreign languages, the social sciences, history, and foreign cultures. Each student spends roughly a quarter of his or her classes taking cores, but the university has considered eliminating the core in recent years.

and pulled out her white Chanel halter bikini. She sighed. Two months of hard work at the **MAC** to prepare for this trip, and all was for naught.

Suddenly, one of the books on her shelf caught her eye. It was *Against Nature*, by Huysmans, a strange book she'd read freshman year. In a triumph of mind over matter, the protagonist of the novel decides to enjoy a sea voyage to England without going to the trouble of actually leaving his house, so he has a room constructed out of timber with portholes for windows, places tinted aquariums outside the portholes, furnishes the room with nautical appointments, sits down and orders an English-style meal, and proceeds to enjoy the illusion of a seaborne vacation.

This gave Parker an idea. In an explosion of clothes, limbs, and hair, she quickly pulled on her bikini and admired her lithe physique in her bedroom mirror.

"If I can't go to the beach," she said to her reflection, "I'll take things poolside."

She slipped into a pair of flip-flops, pulled on her fox-trimmed coat over the bikini, then yanked the plug out of her solar lamp and wrapped the cord around its base. Toting her beach towel, lamp, and a thick romance novel, Parker took the underground passage under B-entryway to get to

MAC: Acronym for Malkin Athletic Center, the main undergrad gym located next to Lowell House.

Adams House pool:
Adams House's indoor swimming pool, where lots of sketchiness once took place. It's since been drained and converted into a theater, as Parker is about to discover.

Radcliffe: Harvard's college for women back in the day when mixed-sex classrooms were considered blasphemous. Now merely an academic institution for the study of women.

the **Adams House pool.** She had always heard the Adams House pool spoken of but had never taken the opportunity to actually visit it. According to legend, decades before it had often been the site for scandalous goings on between Harvard men and their **Radcliffe** ladies.

"It's not the beach," she said to herself as she padded down the stairs to the basement, her flip-flops flapping softly against her heels. "But I guess it'll have to do."

She went through the door and into the basement. She stopped and frowned. There was no blue shimmering water. The room was still labeled ADAMS HOUSE POOL, but all she saw were seats. The pool had been drained and converted into a theater. An empty theater, as no one seemed to be rehearsing or watching on this snowy evening.

Or almost no one, as one figure lay prone on the floor in the center of the stage.

Parker moved nearer. Then she dropped her book, lamp, and towel and screamed.

Hidden Harvard

15 Places You Absolutely *Won't* See on the Campus Tour

Dunster Murder Suite

Site of a brutal murder-suicide in 1995 in which one stressed-out undergrad stabbed her roommate forty-five times with a buck knife and then hanged herself, Dunster's sealed room H-21 is the stuff of myth and legend. The president, friends, and fellows of Harvard College have sealed the room indefinitely until the buzz blows over. In the meantime, just look for that conspicuously large and unmarked "broom closet" between H-20 and H-22.

Dudley Garden

Follow the path between the side entrance of Lamont Library and Wigglesworth A-entryway to discover Harvard's own little secret garden. Technically closed after dark, campus security often forgets to lock the gate at night. Makes a perfect getaway for a little late-night canoodling, though your morning hives and rashes may give you away. "Honestly, Dean, we were just *studying . . .* "

The Fishpond

You'll be hard-pressed to find an undergrad who knows anything about this secret spot. Called the Class of 1959 Chapel and located across the Charles River at the Harvard Business School, this cylindrical/pyramidal building boasts a nondenominational chapel, an out-of-tune harpsichord, and a tiny terraced garden complete with koi.

The Law Library

When tired of complaining about how much work you have to do, get off your ass and actually do some of it. We're tired of hearing about it! Wend your way to the back of the Law School Library, through the dark third-floor international law stacks—all the way to the back, keep going, that's it—to find an enchanted little spare room filled with plush bean bag chairs and lots of natural light. And a faun who serves tea . . .

Memorial Hall's Tower

Ascending the tower of Memorial Hall (aka Annenberg, aka Sander's Theater) will make you recall the final scene of Hitchcock's *Vertigo* with each rotting, wooden, rickety step. Though strictly off-limits, a lucky daring few have found their way up after discovering unlocked access doors. Dank, dusty, dangerous, and downright scary. Rated R.

The Catacombs

Yes, yes, *all* colleges supposedly have labyrinths of steam tunnels running underneath their campuses. Do they really exist? No one knows for sure. Lots of people know people who've met someone who's filmed a documentary down there, but no one can seem to find the damned tape.

The Stadium

Though not exactly hidden, this mammoth, 30,000-seat concrete coliseum is a great place to see the Yale football team get their asses kicked every other year, but an even better place to explore in the dark—the single entrance is never locked. Dare your friends to walk the entire perimeter in the dead of night. Just beware of what—or *who*—lurks in the shadows. Seriously. What's the matter, McFly? Chicken?

Pooh Corner

Pooh Corner is out of the way and often overlooked as students rush between the Yard and the Law School. Oh, bother! Find the little red door marked "Pooh's House" at the base of the tree in the one-acre wood between Littauer and the Science Center.

The Faculty Room

Unless you're one of the thirty or so freshmen who win the prestigious Harvard College scholarship, odds are you will *never* see the faculty room inside University Hall. Rumors abound as to what kinds of treasures this not-so-ordinary teachers' lounge stores—no shabby earth-toned sofas or smelly refrigerators here. Undoubtedly the venue for profs' sexy parties.

Vanserg

Those unlucky enough to have a class in Vanserg Hall at the end of God's green earth will rue the day they ever applied to Harvard—especially when it's winter and −40°F outside. Hastily constructed in the 1950s, this glorified mobile home served as the dumping ground for all of Harvard's unwanted organizations: *V*eterans *A*dministration, *N*aval *S*cience, *E*lectronic *R*esearch, and *G*raduate School. It has somehow escaped the wrecking ball and is without a doubt the *ugliest* thing you will see at Harvard. No wonder it's not on the official tours.

Elmwood

Elmwood is nothing less than Harvard's White House, or in this case, brick house. Since the early 1970s, Harvard presidents have wined here, dined here, slept, showered, shaved, and—well, you get the picture. Only a few lucky students ever see the inside, and then usually only to serve drinks or play elevator music on the staircase landing.

The X-Cage

Although Scully and Mulder kept secret files on aliens and government conspiracies, Harvard's so-called X-Cage holds far more valuable materials: books, photos, paintings, and other smut the university has deemed too pornographic to let anyone see! These materials are supposedly off-limits to everyone except qualified researchers, but they're probably just stashed under some librarian's bed. Keep digging. The truth is out there.

Grays Middle

The second-floor rooms in the middle entryway of Grays Hall are Harvard's "celebrity suites" for famous frosh too important—or just too *scared*!—to live with their plebeian classmates. Supposedly outfitted with bulletproof glass and a panic button with a direct link to the Feds.

Three

Parker stared in horror at the sight in front of her. Shaking, she leaned against the doorway and tried to blink everything away. Once, twice . . . it wasn't working.

This can't be happening, she thought to herself.

A corpse was stretched out across the center of the little stage. But this wasn't the sort of corpse the cops find at the beginning of a *Law and Order* episode. This corpse looked like it had undergone some bizarre and terrifying ritual and been posed as if for its final rest. It was a man in his early twenties, with pale skin and spiky black hair, dressed in the nondescript jeans and hoodie of a typical student. Jutting a full six inches out of his chest was a thick wooden stake with a curving metal design wrapping around its handle. Dark pools of blood trickled down from the wound, and the corpse's eyes were wide open, staring vacantly at Parker. Its mouth was stuffed with something that looked to Parker like garlic, though the thought of looking more closely at it made her stomach turn.

Parker suddenly gasped. She had forgotten to breathe.

As her chest heaved with huge gulps of cold, musty air, she gagged on the overpowering smell of blood, but then she began to overcome her paralysis, sprinting out of the pool room and through the underground tunnel. Before she could even make her way up the stairs to the dining hall, she crashed head on into her friend and former English tutor, J. Z. Crowther, who was carrying a coffee mug. His blue eyes were slightly bloodshot, and his thick, light brown hair was attractively tousled, as if he'd been running his hands through it as he paced the empty halls. Whatever was in the mug went flying, most of it landing on Parker's coat. Whatever it was, it wasn't coffee.

"What the hell's the matter with you, Parker?" growled J. Z., irked about losing his beverage, which smelled strongly of licorice. Parker gaped awkwardly at him, unable to speak. "Hey, you look white as a ghost. Here, swallow what's left of this."

Parker took the mug from J. Z. and took several long gulps. An intensely painful burning sensation pervaded her mouth and throat, making her eyes water and her nose run, but it slowly gave way to a warm, rosy glow. Feeling calmer, Parker steadied herself by putting a hand on his shoulder.

"Call. Security. Now."

"What?"

"Call," she said, grabbing the mug again. "What the hell is this stuff, anyway? Never mind. Call right now. Phone. Phone. Gimme the phone."

"I'll call, OK?" grumbled J. Z. "And that stuff you're drinking is called Arak. It's a traditional Lebanese beverage distilled from wild grapes and flavored with anise. It means 'sweat' in Arabic. I drink it when I'm having trouble sleeping."

"I need to sit," Parker said, slumping to the floor. "I need to sit and think."

J. Z. Crowther was the kind of guy who could keep cool—if **somewhat irritable**—in any situation. He was part of a rare breed of Harvard kids who were certifiable geniuses but would never let on to it. When he told Parker that he was admitted to **Phi Beta Kappa** in the spring, she was floored. She knew he was sharp, but not once in the entire time she had known him had she ever seen him sit down with a book to do homework. Instead, J. Z. preferred to roam the halls of Adams House with a mug full of . . . something mysterious and a word of good advice for anyone who sought it. He would have been just as loved by the university's English Department as Neesa Barnett if they hadn't resented his lack of caring for the subject and his unwillingness to indulge in theoretical verbosity. But it wasn't that he didn't care about English, or lectures, or sections; he didn't really care about *anything* in particular. Whereas nearly every male at Harvard would have killed to have had the opportunity to join a **Final Club**, J. Z. turned down invitations from the Spee, Fox, Owl, Fly, and

somewhat irritable: Harvard students can often be a bit . . . irritable. You learn to roll with it. Conquering astrophysics and learning to be a concert pianist doesn't leave these people a lot of time to master their social skills.

Phi Beta Kappa: The national academic honor society—approximately the top 1 percent of college grads in America. Considering the competition, it's a pretty big deal if you're inducted into the society from Harvard.

Final Club: Instead of fraternities and sororities, Harvard has Final Clubs, the epitome of elitism and good-old-boy camaraderie that continues to distinguish the Ivy League to this day.

even the Porcellian during his sophomore year in exchange for a quiet life at Adams House. He was a mystery. And for these reasons, J. Z. was one of Parker's very favorite people at Harvard.

* * * * *

Harvard police:
Harvard University Police Department (HUPD). A friendly lot with their own riot gear.

Kronauer space:
The dark, sketchy little theater under F-entryway that serves as the venue for Adamsites' artsy-fartsy, off-off-off-off-off-off-Broadway productions. Better known as the summer storage room.

When the **Harvard police** arrived, Parker and J. Z. made their way down the stairs, entered the underground hallway, and passed through the **Kronaeur space**. Parker grabbed a fake tree branch (a leftover prop from the latest poorly attended production of *Into the Woods*) and shielded herself behind J. Z. as he led the pack toward the pool theater, coffee mug still in hand. J. Z. took a grim swig of the milky, burning liquid as the others followed closely behind him. Although the corridors were lit by flickering fluorescent lights, Parker couldn't help but feel like it wasn't light enough, and wished that they had thought to bring flashlights along with them. And baseball bats. Or a big stick.

"Right over th—Oh . . . Oh no." Parker pointed, dumbfounded.

The body was gone.

As If!

8 Harvard Myths
Debunked

Big Brother Is Watching . . .

Ever since Harvard alum Ted Kaczynski unabombed his way to the top of America's most-wanted list, the FBI has opened a permanent file on each incoming Harvard frosh. This rumor, however, is just not true. The CIA keeps the files.

Harvard Homeless

The numerous homeless people in Harvard Square are supposedly all college alums who just didn't make it and/or failed freshman calculus. Who the *hell* came up with this? Obviously one of those soulless psychos or premeds. No wonder the rest of the world thinks Harvard kids are spoiled little brats.

The John Harvard Statue

Every tour guide will tell you that students rub the shiny foot of the John Harvard statue for good luck before taking tests and that tourists should rub it too to help their family members get in. Yep, it's true, if by "rub" you mean "pee on" and by "before a test" you mean "at 4 A.M. when the cops aren't around." So rub that foot. Rub it good.

The Science Center Camera

Built in the 1970s with donations from the Harvard-dropout founder of Polaroid, the mammoth science center supposedly looks like a giant camera from the sky. Yeah, right. The only thing this beast resembles is a prison. With computer labs.

Ice Cream in the Dorms

After Harvard alum Harry Elkins Widener died on the *Titanic*, his mommy donated a small fortune to build Widener Library on the condition that the dining halls serve ice cream every day because it'd been Harry's favorite food. Bogus. The dining hall only serves ice cream on Sundays, forcing kids to live off that drippy fro-yo crap Monday through Saturday.

Swim Test

Harry's demanding mum also forced Harvard to administer mandatory swim tests, believing that her son had died because he couldn't swim. Stooooooooopid. Like swimming could've saved the poor bastard. Didn't she see Leo freeze to death in the movie? Duh! Harvard and other schools actually instituted swim tests at the urging of the American Red Cross in the 1920s.

Grade Inflation

Although the national media has been harping about grade inflation at Harvard these past few years, we challenge any of these pundits to actually take a Harvard class and score an A. Go on, we dare you. You can talk the talk, but can you walk the walk? A's only come from sweat, perseverance, and a helluva lot of studying, so is it really hard to believe that a university full of smart, hardworking kids will often receive top grades?

Green Acres

University professors—the handful of the brightest and most renowned Harvard professors—still have the right to graze their cows in Harvard Yard. Hahahahahahahaha! Who comes up with crap like this? That's the kind of cowpie only a Yalie could step in. Oh wait, this one's actually true.

CHAPTER

Four

"I already told you," said a weary Parker, slumped against the wall of the pool theater. "I walked into the room. I saw him lying over there. He had a wooden stake jutting out of his chest, like a vampire that had been staked. I swear, Officer, I'm not making this up. **I do go to Harvard, you know.**"

Sanchez, one of the two HUPD officers who had answered the call, did not look happy.

"The problem is," he said, "in order to report a murder, we really have to have a body." He paused. "Is that liquor?"

Parker looked down at her stained coat, which reeked of alcohol.

"I haven't been drinking," she said firmly. "Someone spilled Arak on my coat—a traditional Lebanese beverage distilled from grapes and flavored with anise."

"I do go to Harvard, you know.": Telling someone else that you go to Harvard to win some respect is known as "dropping the H-bomb." It's great for meeting non-Harvard girls but apparently doesn't work on cops.

Officer Sanchez snorted. "Harvard kids. They even gotta drink different. In my day we drank Crystal Light and Nikolai—everyone got retarded, but no one saw any spooky bodies. You realize if this is a prank it's going on your **permanent record**." He took a pocket-size tape recorder out of the inner pocket of his jacket. After fumbling with it for a few seconds, he managed to turn it on. Clearing his throat, he began to speak.

permanent record: As if Officer Sanchez had any say about her permanent record. Typical cop bluster.

"Ahem. This is Officer Sanchez reporting on case number 10324. Drunk girl who thinks there's been a homicide."

"Hey!" yelled Parker.

Officer Sanchez continued.

"Okay. Let's take it nice and slow. Miss Norcross, tell me what you saw."

"Well, I walked into the—"

Officer Sanchez shoved the recording device into Parker's face, nearly smashing her chin in.

"Repeat it louder, please."

Parker cautiously approached the recorder and, while wearily looking both officers in the eyes, continued her story. She coughed.

"Ahem. Well, like I told you before, I walked into the Adams Pool Theater, and the first thing I saw when I turned on the light was—"

"The Wolfman?" offered Officer Nikita, Sanchez's female partner.

Officer Sanchez burst out laughing.

"Oh man . . . that's classic," he guffawed, wiping a tear from his eye. "All right, all right, let's continue." He snickered. "What did you see again, Buffy? I mean—Miss Norcross?"

This is hopeless, she thought. *Maybe they're right. Maybe I saw something that just wasn't there. But—it seemed so real.*

"WHAT THE HELL IS WRONG WITH YOU PEOPLE!?" screamed J. Z. "Why aren't you searching for FORENSIC EVIDENCE? I should be asleep right now. It's bad enough I have this crippling insomnia. Now I have to stay up half the night listening to YOU morons?"* He was practically apoplectic.

J. Z. looked at Parker, and Parker smiled back at him, wanly. She was grateful for the support, but she wished he wasn't here to see her being humiliated like this. If there was one thing Parker hated worse than being scared, it was **being wrong.**

"Is that all you want, officers?" Parker said resignedly. "It's midnight, and I don't like being here any more than you do."

"Tell me about it," started Officer Nikita,

* Well, okay. Let's add self-absorption and outright bitchiness to the list of common Harvard character traits. Like we said, you learn to look past these trivialities.

being wrong: Every Harvard student's worst nightmare.

pointing to Parker's stained coat, "I'll take a tumbler full of whatever *she's* having, if you know what I mean."

The two officers laughed heartily and continued to do so even after a very frantic-looking Sean Palfrey, the **house master**, ran into the room, followed by his wife, Judith, the other house master. Both of them had forgotten to change out of their pajamas.

house master:
A professor and his/her significant other in charge of an undergraduate house. Impressive title, cushy job.

"What's going on here, officers? Is there any trouble?"

"Oh, it's nothing a little pizza and Gatorade won't help," said Officer Sanchez, grinning at Parker. "She thought she saw a ghost."

"A vampire," mumbled Parker. "It was a vampire. A dead one."

"A HOMICIDE, for Christ's sake," screamed J. Z. in exasperation.

"Oh dear!" said Mr. Palfrey, "I certainly hope it wasn't anything too serious."

"No," said Officer Nikita. "If it was, I suggest calling the Cambridge police next time. But, for something like this, we're happy to help in any way we can."

Parker's ears perked up at the mention of the Cambridge police. The only time she had ever heard of the Cambridge Police Department interfering in the lives of Harvard undergraduates during the past four years was when a shooting was reported outside of Mather House, near the Charles River. All students came to understand during their time at Harvard that the Cambridge police meant business: wherever they were, you didn't want to be there. Unlike HUPD, the Cambridge Police Department wouldn't let you off with a slap on the wrist; if you were actually caught, you stood the chance of spending the night in jail, or worse, the chance of being sent to the **Ad Board**.

"Officers, we can take care of it from here. So sorry to disturb you," said Mr. Palfrey.

Officers Sanchez and Nikita walked out of D-entryway and back into the blizzard. J. Z. exhaled a sigh of relief and walked up to stand by Parker.

"Are you okay, Parker?" asked Master Palfrey.

"I'm fine, Sean. I just thought that—"

"I know, dear. This storm has got us all hearing things. But maybe if you have a warm cup of milk like your friend J. Z. over there"— J. Z. rolled his eyes and muttered some imprecation under his breath—"you'll be able to get some sleep."

Ad Board: Every Harvard student's *other* worst nightmare, the Administrative Board is the body that handles all undergraduate affairs, most notoriously discipline.

"Don't worry, Mr. and Mrs. Palfrey. I'll make sure she gets taken care of," said J. Z. Then, under his breath, "because it's so easy to get to sleep around here."

* * * * *

Parker peeped through the basement window and watched the two HUPD cars drive off into the night. She shivered. There was no doubt in her mind that she had seen the body. But . . . where was it now? If it were really a **prank**, why would they only target her?

Parker was so deep in thought that when J. Z. came up behind her she gasped.

"I'm sorry about this, J. Z.," Parker said. "You didn't have to wait here for me. You should get back to bed. I just . . . I'm just so sure of what I saw."

"Like there's any *point* in going back to bed," J. Z. wailed in despair. "Don't you *understand*? Haven't you been *listening*? I haven't been able to fall asleep in weeks. I have this debilitating insomnia—it's killing me. Look, why don't I walk you back to your room?"

Parker looked up at J. Z. warmly.

"Thanks, but after all of this, I don't really

prank: Like college students everywhere, Harvard students have always enjoyed pulling pranks, and the houses, Final Clubs, and campus publications prank each other regularly.

feel like sleeping in the house tonight. I'm going to try to book a hotel room at the **Charles** and hope that the airport will reopen in the morning so I can get the hell out of here."

J. Z. sighed, exhausted, his eyes red. "Fine. I'll wait with you until you can get a reservation."

Parker grinned. "How could I say no?"

Charles: The Charles Hotel—one of the ritzy Harvard Square hotels that go for about $500 a night.

* * * * *

After she got back to her room, Parker grabbed her cell phone and sat down at her desk, while J. Z. took a seat on her common room futon with the romance novel that Parker had left behind in the pool theater—*The Cowboy*, by Joan Johnston.

There were no rooms available at the Charles. She dialed the **Inn at Harvard**, the Harvard Square Hotel, the Radisson, and even the Central Square Hilton. No luck. As a last resort, she tried the Cambridge Bed and Muffin. Straight to an answering machine.

Inn at Harvard: Another expensive hotel just outside Harvard Yard, which is rumored to be on its way to becoming a frosh dorm in the very near future.

She trotted into the living room to tell J. Z. the bad news and found him engrossed in *The Cowboy*. He raised his bloodshot eyes from the book.

"No luck?"

CHAPTER FOUR | 44
CHAPTER FOUR | 44

"All the hotels are booked," she said. "I know this sounds sort of weird, but would you mind sleeping out here tonight? You know, to keep me company?"

"*Sleeping*?" J. Z. shrieked. "How do you expect me to *sleep* on this lumpy futon with *vampires* roaming free through the building?! It's bad enough I've got this *insomnia* on a normal basis, now I have to deal with this Hannibal Lecter crap?"

"Just try to rest, J. Z.," Parker said.

"Fine," he muttered, his head drooping onto a pink throw pillow.

Parker patted his shaggy brown hair and began to walk back to her bedroom. She paused in the doorway for a moment and walked back to the futon J. Z. was sitting on. With a rough shove, she pushed the futon across the room, barricading the main door to her room.

"WHAT THE HELL DO I LOOK LIKE— *a freaking shuffleboard puck?!*"*

"Sorry!"

She wasn't about to take any chances.

* Oh, give it a rest, J. Z. We're not making any more excuses for you.

* * * * *

Parker heard the faint noises of J. Z. flipping pages and muttering to himself in the next room. Although she might normally be annoyed at his ranting, it was an odd comfort to her now. She closed her eyes and began to fall into a deep sleep.

Until she was jolted awake by a piercing scream.

Harvard: A History

20 Episodes of Riot and Rabble-Rousing

Despite the stereotype of stuffiness and conservatism, Harvard has (almost) always been a bastion of liberalism. Consequently, students and professors alike have had a long history of feistiness, dissent, riotousness, and all-out rebellion.

1636: The Founding

Harvard became the first college in America in 1636 when nine students enrolled under the tutelage of Master Nathaniel Eaton, a diehard Puritan who instilled the fear of God in his students by beating the crap out of them. Thank you, sir! May I have another?! Eaton lasted only a year until a Cambridge jury fired him—ironically, for serving bad food.

1675: The Hoar Rebellion

Students apparently hated Harvard President Leonard Hoar so much that they boycotted classes and just left campus, forcing Hoar to resign and the college to close for several months. Thus was launched a glorious tradition of telling The Man to shove it.

1725: Mather Mayhem

When the university refused to administer mandatory religious exams, Harvard President Increase Mather and his son Cotton declared the school wicked and godless. They fled Cambridge and committed the most heinous crime imaginable: they helped found Yale. Increase and Cotton will always be remembered for their treachery and their ridiculous names.

1765: The Rebellion Tree

In support of Boston's Sons of Liberty and to protest the hated British Stamp Act, Harvard College students christened a tree in the Yard the "Rebellion Tree," which served as the sight for many effigy hangings and student protests over the next century.

1766: The Butter Rebellion

Pissed that the food still sucked, Harvard men walked out of classes.

1768: The Recitation Rebellion

Students rioted again in 1768, after a new rule forbade them from putting off their required recitation exams. They smashed windows, threw poop at the tutors (not their own, we hope), and—*gasp!*—even threatened to transfer to Yale!

1776: Washington and the War

George Washington conducted the first months of the Revolutionary War from Cambridge and ordered Harvard to remove students from the frosh dorms in the Yard so that he could house his troops there. Harvard laughed and told him he'd have to share with the frosh, a sucky arrangement for both. Peeved, Washington eventually set up shop on nearby Brattle Street.

1805: The Bread and Butter Rebellion

Substandard grub once again prompted college men to boycott classes. Hmm, trend developing.

1807: The Cabbage Rebellion

Okay, definite pattern here. College administrators got so fed up with food-related rebellions that they finally hired a professional chef. Third time's a charm. (Though judging by present dining hall fare, you wouldn't be able to tell!)

1820–1920: Bloody Monday

Sophomores would bludgeon the living daylights out of the new frosh flesh on the first Monday night of every new school year. *Fresh meat tonight, boys!* Too bad they eventually banned this fine, fine tradition.

1823: The Great Rebellion of 1823

When the powers-that-be expelled a Harvard senior shortly before graduation, the entire senior class decided to boycott commencement. Harvard retaliated by expelling more than half the class, but later revised the disciplinary policies with the hope of preventing future embarrassing walkouts. Fat chance!

1834: The Freshman Rebellion

Students rioted with unprecedented violence when Harvard President Josiah Quincy threatened to expel a number of popular freshmen and sophomores for disobedience. They ransacked rooms, smashed windows and furniture, vandalized buildings, and even ignited a bomb in the middle of church. Scores of students, including the entire sophomore class, eventually walked out, prompting more expulsions and the first arrests on campus.

1879: Radcliffe Forms

Disgruntled that they'd been excluded from Harvard, prominent Cambridge women banded together in 1879 to form the "Harvard Annex," later renamed Radcliffe College. Undoubtedly a great source of happiness—and distraction—to the proverbial ten thousand men of Harvard. Finally! An outlet for all their frustrations!

1932: The Bell Riot

Overcome with grief that someone had stolen the clapper from the bell in Memorial Hall's tower, undergrads convened in the Yard to search for their purloined property. They ransacked the frosh suites and then stormed the Radcliffe women's dorms, ostensibly to find the bell, but undoubtedly seeking a little action. The mob then rioted in Harvard Square, forcing local cops to break out the tear gas.

1952: The Pogo Riot

More than a thousand rankled Harvardians took to the streets when the writer of the popular comic strip *Pogo* cancelled an appearance. Cambridge police arrived and dove into the fray, beating some students and arresting two dozen others. Honestly, gentlemen . . . over a comic strip?!

1961: The Diploma Riots

Police used tear gas and handcuffs to dispel a mob of angry seniors who'd marched to university president Nathan Pusey's house to raise hell. Their beef: Harvard had written their diplomas in English instead of the traditional Latin. Lamest excuse for a riot ever.

1969: University Hall Take-Over

Incensed by Harvard's ties to the military during the Vietnam War, a handful of students took matters into their own hands by storming the Yard, forcefully occupying University Hall, and dragging one of the deans down the steps. *Take that! And that! That'll teach you!* More tear gas and mass arrests.

1970: The Harvard Square Riot

Still not satisfied, students in Harvard Square protesting the war a year later turned against cops trying to break up the rally. Local hipsters and the homeless joined in the fray, smashing windows, looting, and beating the crap out of everyone else for the next four hours. Rumpus!

2001: The Living Wage Campaign

With full support from the faculty, roughly fifty students camped on the first floor of Massachusetts Hall outside the president's office for nearly a month to protest Harvard's treatment of its part-time, nonunion employees. All twelve of them. More than a hundred other students camped in the Yard to support the cause. The president eventually caved, probably because he couldn't stand the stink.

2005: Faculty Votes No Confidence

Outraged by Harvard President Larry Summers' leadership style and remarks about women and the sciences, faculty members voted no confidence in Summers, urging him to resign. The faculty has no real say in such matters and the vote was purely symbolic, but it nevertheless marked the first no-confidence vote against a president in the history of Harvard. Oh, and Summers eventually resigned a year later.

CHAPTER
Five

Parker jerked upright in her bed, covered in
sweat. She leaped out of bed and ran into the
room where J. Z. sat, her novel cracked open and
face down on the futon beside him, his reassur-
ingly familiar yellow mug in his hand. "Did you
hear that, J. Z.?"

"OF COURSE I heard it," J. Z. bellowed.
"How the hell do you think I'm going to sleep
with all of this racket? It's bad enough I've got
this insomnia—now I have to deal with these
bloodcurdling screams?"

"But you weren't sleeping *before* the scream?"

"What does it LOOK like?"*   * What *does* it look like?

Before she could answer, they were interrupted by another piercing scream. J. Z. pulled
the futon away from the door, and they ran
down the stairs in the direction of the noise. It
wasn't long before they found its source—the girl
hadn't stopped screaming. When they reached

the room—Adams B-32, Neesa's room—everyone in Adams House was already there.

Jenkins, the **senior tutor**, pushed his way through the crowd. He was wearing a pair of plaid pajama bottoms and a T-shirt that read *F.B.I.: Female Body Inspector.* "Hey! What's going on in there?" he yelled, pounding on the door. "Open up!"

The door swung open to reveal a hysterical Neesa Barnett, covered in blood.

She was pointing a bloody finger at her neck.

It was hard to make out through the blood, but Parker could have sworn she saw two neat puncture holes dotting Neesa's neck. Like two perfectly placed . . . fang marks?

"Neesa," started Jenkins, who had gone white as a sheet and was trembling, "come here, we have to . . . we have to get you to **UHS** right away."

Sobbing, Neesa collapsed into Jenkins's arms. Considering that this was probably the first time in his life that a girl had willingly embraced him, Jenkins was appropriately flabbergasted. He tried to move Neesa along as best he could. She held onto him for dear life.

The two house masters came barreling up the stairs for the second time that evening. Although

senior tutor: The senior tutor is a graduate student or sometimes very low-ranking professor who's in charge of all the students' academic records, signs all the study cards, and keeps the academic files of the residents. He or she lives in the house, but often has an apartment off to the side and isn't involved with students' daily lives. Senior tutors don't eat with the students, supervise house parties, go on house trips, etc. Not to be confused with the regular tutors, who do. Each house has ten to twenty tutors (sort of like RAs in other colleges) but only one senior tutor.

UHS: University Health Services, the unsmartest people on campus. Known to have told male students that they're not pregnant.

they looked a bit groggy, they seemed to be in happier spirits than when Parker last saw them in the pool.

"What is it this time?" joked Sean, pulling his robe tightly around his waist. "Frankenstein?" When he saw the frightened faces of his students, the blood staining the floor, and a tearful and bloodied Neesa clinging to Jenkins, his jaw dropped.

"Oh my God. Oh my God," he repeated over and over. "Poor Neesa!"

Parker glowered in the corner. J. Z. put his hands on her shoulders. Half for comfort, half in case she needed to be physically restrained.

* * * * *

Everyone trickled out of Adams House as the police and paramedics arrived. Although the house masters told everyone to stay inside and go back to their rooms, everyone was anxious to know what had happened to Neesa. Even though she stood at a distance from all the action, Parker could tell this was serious business. Her old friends, Officers Sanchez and Nikita, were there, but so were three other policemen who arrived on the scene in Cambridge police cars. The person—or thing—responsible for harming Neesa was not going to get off easy, student or no.

"Hey you!" hollered Officer Sanchez from a distance. Parker squinted.

"Yeah, you! Buffy! Get over here!" shouted Officer Nikita.

Parker looked at J. Z. He shrugged and followed her as she walked across the street toward the police. They got to the other side in the middle of Neesa's interrogation.

"I was sleeping," sniffled Neesa, "I woke up to find someone leaning over me. He bit me, and then he ran off."

She uncovered the bloody piece of cloth that was covering her neck to expose the two fresh wounds. For the first time since Parker had known her, she felt sorry for Neesa. Whatever discomfort she may have caused Parker in the past, she certainly hadn't deserved this.

One of the Cambridge police officers nodded in Parker's direction.

"Are you Parker Norcross?" he asked.

"I am," she said.

"A little less than six hours ago, you reported a 'vampire slaying' in this same building?"

"Well, yes, sort of."

"But there was no body found?"

"Right. Someone must have moved it."

"Wh-what if it wasn't a corpse?" asked Neesa, turning away from the officers to face Parker. "What if . . . what if whatever you saw . . . is still alive? What if someone tried to kill it for a reason?"

"Neesa, I'm not saying you're wrong," said J. Z. cautiously, "but I think we're all forgetting the most important piece of the puzzle."

"And what's that?"

"THAT THERE'S NO SUCH *THING* AS VAMPIRES! Or had you forgotten?"

"Listen to me, Crowther," she snapped. "I'm being targeted! A *vampire* attack. Maybe I've stirred up something unholy with my thesis research. The thesis of the year at Harvard University—it's going to attract a lot of attention, that's all I'm saying. Maybe someone—or some*thing*—doesn't want that kind of attention."

She started to cry in great, heaving sobs.

The Cambridge police officer looked at her, then to Parker and J. Z., who rolled his eyes.

"Stick around," he said. "Not that you can really go anywhere in this weather. But we may need to talk to you."

The police officers all huddled around Neesa and escorted her to the nearby ambulance. The flashing lights illuminated the surrounding snow banks a deep red that blended into the burgeoning crimson sunrise. Parker and J. Z. watched them walk away, their breath making steamy puffs in the cold morning air.

J. Z. groaned. "Why does everyone keep overemphasizing the word *thing*? 'Someone or some*thing*,' 'the person or *thing* that did this.' *Thing thing thing.* It's driving me crazy. I could be up all night with this word ringing in my head."

"Come on, J. Z. I haven't had a decent meal in days," said Parker. "Let's see what we can find to eat around here."

J. Z. followed her wordlessly as they walked up the snow-covered street. The plows hadn't come by yet. If not for the towering mounds of snow showing where cars had been

Crimson building:
Home of the *Harvard Crimson*, one of America's oldest college daily newspapers.

junior staffers:
Slaves, in other words, forced to do humiliating, menial tasks to some day get a byline.

Harvard Yard: The Yard, as it's more commonly called, is the oldest part of campus. Home to most frosh dorms as well as a variety of classrooms, student organization offices, and administrative buildings.

Crimson, Lampoon, and Advocate: Joining one of these three publications is essential for any aspiring young writer, not so much for the experience but for networking. It's all about whom you know.

parked, ranged in regularly spaced rows like a parade of giant snowmen, the landscape would have resembled a thickly blanketed wilderness.

They passed by the **Crimson building** on the right. Even though it was seven in the morning, the windows of the first and second floor were lit up, which, Parker guessed, meant that one or two wretched **junior staffers** were probably busy at work on their computers, chugging Red Bulls and trying to write a killer story that could raise them to the next stratum in the staff hierarchy.

Parker had always believed that getting into Harvard would be the great reward for all of the long hours she put into her work in high school. She believed that once she made it to the top of her high school class, she would have earned her spot in a university where everyone could be content knowing that they were the best of the best. She couldn't have been more wrong. If anything, the competition got even fiercer once she entered the ivy-decked walls of **Harvard Yard**. It wasn't enough to take the most rigorous advanced-standing classes; you also had to be a part of the elite social organizations, while contributing to as many literary publications as possible. But only the prestigious ones like the ***Crimson, Lampoon,*** and ***Advocate,*** naturally.

If a guy got into the Owl, he was disappointed he didn't get into the Spee. Likewise, if a girl got into the **Sabliere Society**, she complained to her roommates that the **Bee** snubbed her because she was "too good looking." There was always something bigger and better to do, and everyone was fighting tooth and nail for the most coveted spots on—*

"ENOUGH!" J. Z. was screaming again, having somehow read her thoughts. "WHY ARE YOU WASTING VALUABLE NARRATIVE ON THIS SELF-ABSORBED CRAP?! If you didn't want to compete you wouldn't *be here.* You're not supposed to be thinking about the Owl or the Spee—*you're going to get something to eat.* That's your motivation in this scene."

Parker continued with J. Z. down Massachusetts Avenue. Although the snow began to fall thickly around them, she could make out the outline of the Yard across the street.

Parker had fond memories of living in Weld Hall as a freshman. She remembered her first Harvard snowfall, a light dusting compared to the previous day's monster storm. There had still been enough snow to have a respectable snowball fight, and it seemed that everyone in the freshman class was eager to participate, frolicking around **Emerson** and **Widener**, ducking

Sabliere Society and the Bee: All-women Final Clubs. Just not as cool as the real Final Clubs.

* This paragraph was actually written by a self-absorbed Harvard student.

Emerson: A small lecture hall between Sever Hall and Lamont Library devoted to humanities courses. Named after Ralph Waldo himself.

Widener: Widener Library—Harvard's main branch named after an alum who died on the Titanic—is located smack in the middle of Harvard Yard and houses more than 3 million volumes on a dozen floors of open stacks. Widener has more security than Fort Knox, leading some students to grumble (only half-jokingly) that Harvard cares more about its books than its students.

John Harvard statue: Supposedly one of the most photographed statues in the world, good ol' John Harvard is the centerpiece of Harvard Yard, inscribed with the words "John Harvard, founder, 1638." For this reason, it's commonly referred to as the Statue of Three Lies: the college was founded in 1636 and changed it's named when John Harvard donated his personal library. And since no portraits of Johnny have survived, the statue's face was actually modeled after a resident freshman in 1884. Students pee on it.

Greenhouse Café: Cozy little diner smack dab in the middle of Harvard Square, with the best bacon cheeseburgers in town. Also has a satellite mini-diner in the Science Center.

behind trees. But never near the **John Harvard statue.** Parker certainly had many fantastic times living in the Yard. But now, after all that had happened, the Yard looked like an unfriendly and foreboding place.

Shaking it off, she continued with J. Z. down Mass. Ave until they reached her favorite late night/early morning hangout—the **Greenhouse Café.** The moment they walked through its doors, Parker exhaled a sigh of relief. The smell of pancakes and frying bacon hung thick in the air. Thick slices of cake glistened invitingly through the pastry display case near the register. Parker mentally selected the slice that she would take home with her after the meal was over.

The hostess sat Parker and J. Z. in a small table near the window. Although the restaurant was usually packed on weekday mornings, it was rather empty today, probably because the snow from the storm hadn't been cleared. As Parker slid into her chair, she tried to reach for her water but ended up knocking it over. As she righted the glass, she noticed that her hands were shaking.

"J. Z., what the hell is happening here?" She fought to keep her voice calm but mostly failed. With the most placid expression Parker had seen him wearing in recent memory, J. Z. calmly mopped up the spill with a handful of paper napkins. The waitress came over with a fresh glass of water, but J. Z. waved her away with an impatient gesture.

"J. Z., what are you doing? Can't you see this is serious?" Parker's frayed nerves were starting to give way to anger as she watched him fiddling with the glass.

J. Z. silenced her with a quick shake of his head. He shook her empty water glass out over the floor, ridding it of its last few drops. Then he set it upright in front of her, pulled a tall bottle with a blue cap out of his satchel, and started to pour in a clear liquid that turned milky when it hit the glass.

"More Arak? J. Z., it's like seven A.M. I hardly—"

"Actually, it's **Rakı**, from Turkey. Distilled from figs. It originated in the Ottoman Empire."

"Another sleep aid?"

"Just drink it."

As she sipped, her mouth and throat were filled with an overpowering searing sensation, as if she'd swallowed lye. She wiped her nose with a napkin and squeezed tears out of her eyes. Finally, the burning sensation gave way to a feeling of warmth, pervading her chest and radiating out through her extremities, giving rise to a sense of deep and abiding well-being.

Rakı: Extremely popular beverage among Harvard students who—oh, never mind.

After a moment, J. Z. broke into her reverie. "You were saying, Parker?"

"Oh. Right. What do you think is actually going on here? I mean, a body that's been staked like a vampire and then a quote-unquote *vampire attack*? It's a bit much to swallow, don't you think? So I'm thinking maybe the whole thing is a sick hoax, but I can't really buy that, because I was *there*. That body was *dead*. And it wasn't just how it looked—I could *smell* the blood. It made me gag. And then that creepy stake, with its weird design, like something from a satanic ritual. But if it wasn't a hoax, and it's not slayers and vampires, someone committed a murder and an aggravated assault. Some psycho—and that's just as bad as having a vampire in the house. And what does this psychopath think he is—a vampire slayer or a vampire? Or does he have a split personality?"

"Slow down, Parker. Think about what we *do* know. You said the stake had a design. Do you remember what it looked like?"

Parker thought for a moment. "Yes, sure—but it's not like anything I've ever seen before." J. Z. raised his eyebrows expectantly. "It looked like a snake, wrapping around the handle. It seemed . . . old."

"Could you draw it?"

"I think so."

"Maybe we could find something out about it based on . . ." He trailed off.

"What? What is it?"

"Isn't that Dunston Peck over there? Since when does he come out of his room?"

Parker looked, and sure enough Dunston was following the waitress toward a table at the far end of the diner, shielding his pale face with his hand as if the light hurt him. "Yes, that's definitely him." Dunston had picked up his water glass and was turning it back and forth quizzically, as if he were examining it for impurities.

J. Z. leaned forward eagerly. "Dunston's an anthropology concentrator, right?" Parker nodded, leaning forward too. "He knows all kinds of creepy stuff—human sacrifices and rituals and all of that. Maybe that design will mean something to him. DUNSTON!" he screamed. "Dunston, get over here. Yes, you." Dunston was pointing to himself, clearly taken aback at being addressed in this rough fashion.

Parker flinched. "But J. Z., I don't trust him. What if he Hannibal Lecters me?"

"What if he what?"

"You know how creepy he is. He tried to feed me organ meats out of his refrigerator. What if he tries to exchange what he knows for some creepy quid pro quo, like making me tell him about the day I first got my period?* I'm telling you, he's a *ghoul.*—" She broke off, as Dunston had materialized at their table faster than she had expected.

"Um, I believe my presence was wanted here?

* This is *exactly* the sort of thing a Harvard student would do.

May I be of some service?" Dunston had drawn his skinny body up to its full height and was rubbing his hands together awkwardly, like a praying mantis. He made a clicking noise with his mouth.

"Dunston, stop clicking at us and sit down," J. Z. snapped. Dunston hesitated, eyes widening as if he'd like to eat J. Z., but he did as told. "Now, we want to know if, in your investigations of the material culture of insane and barbaric violence, you might have seen a wooden stake with a serpent design. Here, Parker will show you."

Parker sketched the design on a napkin with a blue ballpoint pen and slid it across to Dunston, who looked at it and furrowed his brow.

"And where did you see this?" he asked.

Parker hesitated, then took the plunge. "On a wooden stake, sticking out of that guy's chest who I found in the pool. And don't even tell me I imagined it, okay?"

Dunston smiled, rubbing his hands together. "Yes, I heard about that. Perhaps I can be of some small assistance, yes. Though you ran out of my room so suddenly the other day, my dear. And so you want my help, now, hmmm. Perhaps you should come up to my rooms for tea while we discuss it, hmmm? Perhaps there's something you might do for me in return, a little quid pro quo, yes?"

Parker kicked J. Z. under the table.

Suddenly, J. Z. reached across the table and plucked the water glass out of the hands of Dunston, who looked at him in amazement.

"Hey, I was drinking that, my good fellow."

"No, you weren't." J. Z. reached around Parker's back and dumped the glass's contents into a potted plant on the windowsill. Then he went back into his satchel for the bottle and poured a measure out into the glass before sliding it across the table to Dunston. "Stop talking for a minute and drink this."

"My good man, I hardly think—"

"It's from Turkey. Think of it as an anthropological experiment."

Dunston took the glass, nervously. At a threatening look from J. Z., he downed the harsh liquor in a single gulp.

Then he coughed what little he hadn't swallowed all over Parker and J. Z.

"Heavens, I'm sorry, my dears, I . . . I can't breathe!" Parker pounded him on the back as his face turned red. He gulped for air. After a minute or two, he calmed down and smiled at them both.

"Well, now, that *is* better! Good heavens. I've never before imbibed beverages of a spirituous order—my lord! Miss Norcross, Master Crowther—I feel, I feel such *warmth* and tenderness toward you both. I never saw what friends you really were. When I reconvene with my aging mother and admittedly somewhat sickly sister at our house in Rhode Island next Halloween, I do so hope you'll join us. Mother can be somewhat cruel, but I'm sure she'd have no objection to extending hospitality to two such capital—"

"*Dunston!*" It was the third time Parker had tried to

interrupt him. "I'm happy that we're all friends, but . . . the pattern? Did you recognize it?"

"Oh, it's Celtic, clearly. I should say the style is late *La Tène* period."

"You mean the stake is Irish?"

"Well, aha, hmm, yes, I wouldn't say that exactly. The Celts were once spread all across Europe—France, Germany. The Gauls were Celts. And in the second place, that couldn't have been a stake."

"What the hell do you mean? Of course it was a stake. That guy was stabbed through the flipping heart, for God's sake."

"The Celts didn't decorate stakes—and, ahem, they didn't impale people. They weren't savages, you know. It *does* sound like a spear—though only a fragment, clearly."

"What are you talking about, Dunston? This guy was stabbed by a stake that wasn't a stake? That makes no sense." Then, since Dunston only shrugged, she said, "So what is it for?"

"I have no idea, my dear."

"Well, can you look it up? Is there some way we could find out, like, now?"

"Glenn could answer your question. Glenn Maxwell. Except I'm afraid he's in Ireland for the semester."

Parker rolled her eyes in exasperation as she considered whether another shot of Rakı might help things along. What good was it to her to find out there was this guy who *could* help her . . . *if* he weren't studying abroad?

"He went to Ireland to prove that Dracula is actually

buried there."

"He what?!" Parker spluttered, practically choking.

"He went to Ireland to prove that Dracula is buried there. Well, not *that* Dracula—not Vlad Tepes of Transylvania. That horrible tyrant may have been a bloodthirsty murderer, but he wasn't actually a vampire—at least, not according to Glenn."

"Wait—you're telling me you know a guy at Harvard who's obsessed with some vampire theory and who knows about Celtic designs like the one I saw?" Parker shot a look at J. Z., who seemed deep in thought. "Dunston, are you sure he's actually gone?"

"Quite sure, Miss Norcross. I took him to the airport myself. He hasn't been here in months."

J. Z. suddenly cut in. "What's all this about Dracula being Irish, Dunston?"

"Well, no doubt you know that Bram Stoker was Irish. As was Joseph Sheridan Le Fanu, his illustrious predecessor, the author of *Carmilla*. Both may have set their stories in Eastern Europe, but neither had ever been there. The villages, the peasants, the ruined castles, rural life—all of that was taken from their experiences in Ireland. What's more, the legends of the vampire that were the basis of their fiction were all Irish, not Romanian."

"What legends?"

"Well, my dears, the oldest recording of a vampire concerned a Celtic chieftain named Abhartach. Abhartach was so cruel to his own people that they persuaded Cathan, a rival chieftain, to come and kill him, but the day after he was buried he came back with a basin and made all of his subjects pour blood into it from their wrists for him to drink. Cathan kept slaying him, but he kept coming back with his awful bowl, until finally Cathan consulted a druid, who—if you're as big a *Buffy* fan as me and Glenn—you might say was the first Watcher ever recorded. Though this druid's name has not survived."

"And what did the druid say to do?" asked Parker. "Did it at least involve a spear?"

"Well, no. The druid said to bury Abhartach vertically but upside down, to place a large stone over the grave, to plant thorns around the stone, and to tend the thorns carefully. Glenn thought he'd found the spot in North Derry, Ireland, where Abhartach was supposedly buried, and he went there to see for himself whether the stone and the thorns were still in order, you see."

"But what set him off on this quest during this particular semester?"

"Oh, it was reading Elizabeth Kostova's *The Historian*. Glenn *loathed* that book. She's a graduate of Yale, you know. The book just infuriated him with its inaccuracies—characters running all over the former Ottoman Empire, looking for Dracula in Istanbul, Romania, Hungary, Bulgaria. All of that was just Bram Stoker's smokescreen—for Ireland!"

"You realize he *must* have something to do with these attacks, right?" put in Parker.

"Well, actually, no, my dear. It seems to me that everything about the attack you described, and the attack on Miss

Barnett, seems to point away from dear Glenn."

"What do you mean?" Parker asked, impatiently.

"The use of a stake to stab someone through the heart. That's not the way Abhartach was killed, certainly, and Glenn would have considered it fanciful nonsense. And then the biting on the neck—it makes no sense. Glenn always said—and he's pestered the med students incessantly on this—that a bite on the jugular would simply kill a person more or less immediately. They wouldn't linger through three separate attacks before dying—they'd just bleed to death right away."

"Neesa didn't die right away."

"I can't help you there, my dear. I have no idea what happened to Neesa. But Glenn was a stickler, and he knew the historical record. A cut on the wrist or the breast might be good sources of blood, but never the neck."

Parker and J. Z. looked at each other across the table for a moment. Finally, J. Z. spoke up.

"Where was Glenn's dorm room, Dunston?"

Dunston rubbed his hands together and smiled. The answer, when it came, was as chilling as it was brief.

"Mather."

The Freshman 15

15 Classes Freshmen Usually Take

With the exception of Expos and maybe a foreign language, freshmen are rarely *required* to take any classes. Nevertheless, most frosh end up taking a number of these first-year staples.

Expos

No matter how many books you've published, how many Pulitzers you've won, or how many essays you've written for *The New Yorker*, everyone *has* to take Expository Writing. Be prepared for crappy preceptors who couldn't get tenure-track teaching jobs anywhere else. Take comfort in the advice that many famous Harvard profs impart to their saddened students: "Remember what you learned in Expos. Then forget it."

Ec 10

Harvard's largest class with more than 800 students per year, Social Analysis 10 (aka Economics 10, or simply Ec 10) is also one of the school's few yearlong courses. The instructor is a staunch conservative and the exams are brutal, but don't cry, the curve is low so everyone passes. Prereq for economics and social studies concentrators.

Spanish

Fuelled with the hope of graduating with a fluency citation or merely to pass the foreign language proficiency requirement, hundreds of freshmen take Spanish every year. Most start with the yearlong Spanish A intro, some with the semester-long intermediate Spanish Ca, but all promptly forget it after test day.

Math

Most frosh sign up for some kind of math—be it calculus, multivariable calc, or linear algebra—and then regret it after their non–English-speaking teaching fellow tries to explain why they failed their first hourly exam. Yeah, good luck with that. Prereq for all premeds, science, math, statistics, economics, and computer science concentrators.

Gov 10

Plato. Locke. Marx. Weber. You'll learn to love 'em or love to hate 'em in this introduction to political philosophy course that so many future government concentrators take and later regret. Word to the wise: gov concentrators don't even have to take it!

Hist 10b

The thrilling sequel to History 10a. Known as Western Civ, part two, anywhere else. Fortunately, only a prereq for history and social studies concentrators.

Freshman Seminars

Ever thought about the physics of boat wakes? Or wanted to know the history of zoos? Or what the hell poets are really for? Here's your chance to answer all these and other pressing questions that keep you awake each night. Eclectic but popular, many freshman choose to take these frosh-only classes for fun. Highly recommended.

CS 50

Simply put, Computer Science 50 is hell in a nutshell. Calling it challenging just wouldn't do it justice. Looks great on any résumé—if you don't fail. Prereq for all computer science concentrators.

Psych 1

Fluffy and fun, Psychology 1 makes a great gut to lighten the course load. Sadly, however, it'll make you realize just how much you resemble that little rat racing frantically through the maze. Prereq for all psychology concentrators.

Science B-29: Sex

Officially titled Evolution of Human Behavior, but commonly known as just "Sex," B-29 is every freshman's dream: sex, sex, and more sex. People sex, monkey sex, whale sex—you'll never get your fill. Science porn. Prereq for some psychology, computer science, philosophy, and neurobiology students.

Moral Reasoning 22: Justice

One of the most popular cores, Justice is a good place to ponder life's questions but a horrible spot for a catnap. You'll feel like you're on an episode of *The Price Is Right* as Prof. Michael Sandel walks through the audience getting student input in the middle of lectures. Come on down!

Chem 5

Since most frosh have delusions of medical school, most take Chem 5. And then more chem. Then more chem their sophomore year. You'll be so sick of electron orbitals, hydroxyls, benzene rings, long hours in the lab, and worrying about the ferocious curve that writing those Expos papers will be a welcome break. Prereq for all premed, science, environmental science, and public policy concentrators.

Stats 100

A boring, boring, *boring* class that lots of students waste an elective on because they think it'll be useful someday. You'll probably choose to take it anyway, though, despite the warning. Prereq for all stats concentrators.

English 10a

Aspiring novelists, poets, and essayists usually start out with English 10a and English 10b, aka British Writers I and II. Lots of authors, even more novels, and too many characters to shake a fist at. Aaaugh!! Relax: www.sparknotes.com. *SmarterBetterFaster.* Prereq for all English concentrators.

Biological Sciences 50

Many frosh hoping to get a head start on those premed requirements take BS 50, the aptly named introduction to genetics. Play Watson and Crick with your buddies in style, just like you've always wanted. No boring *Drosphilidae* here.

Six

Parker was talking to J. Z. excitedly as they walked across the street away from the diner.

"Well, that certainly explains a lot. Why we've never seen this guy who's been going to school with us for three years. Plus, why he went crazy and started biting and killing people. He lives in Mather."

"I'd have to agree with you there, Park. Those people are so isolated that for them, deciding you're a vampire and going on a murderous rampage would actually be pretty mild behavior. You remember that Cracraft kid . . ."

Located at Cowperthwaite and Banks Streets, separated from Adams by a bend in the **Charles River** and usually accessible only by **shuttle** or helicopter, Mather House was the farthest removed of all the dorms from the center of campus. Except for the **Quad**, of course—which is so isolated it doesn't even enter into this equation.

Charles River: The river that runs through Boston and past Cambridge. Loaded with toxic sludge. The Charles is also the venue for the Head of the Charles Regatta, when crew teams from universities around the world row head to head every year.

shuttle: The bus that makes the long, treacherous journey between the Science Center and Mather. Not the space shuttle.

Quad: Short for the Radcliffe Quadrangle, the sight of the old Radcliffe College for women. So far away from Harvard Yard that it might as well be in the next state.

Harvard Coop: The 125-year-old campus bookstore that's now semi-secretly managed by Barnes & Noble.

Actually, it's not that much of a secret that the Harvard Coop is a Barnes & Noble. It doesn't have B&N bags or signs or anything, but the little things give it away. Like all those "Barnes & Noble" stickers on the remaindered books on the bargain tables. Or all the books published by Barnes & Noble that it stocks there. We're smart kids, and we actually live here, so . . . we know. And secretly, we like our campus Barnes & Noble just fine.

The Harvard Coop has a café, too, like most Barnes & Nobles. It's a tiny one in the back of the second floor/mezzanine level of the bookstore part of it. You actually have to want to go to the café—you can't just stumble upon it—because it's wedged behind the spiral staircase in this little triangular area. It serves all the same stuff any B&N cafe would: cheese pretzels, scones, cheesecake factory cakes, and big-ass peanut butter–chocolate chip cookies. But it's better because it's clandestine—no one's supposed to know it's a B&N café, so it feels pleasantly naughty to go there.

Come to think of it, it's always packed with young people who are studying, but no one seems to know who those kids are. Given the fact that there are far more grad students at Harvard than undergrads, they're probably grad students since they're all much better dressed than the grubby undergrads. But wait—that can't be it. Since when are grad students well dressed? We may have unwittingly stumbled upon a

"We're going to have to break into his room, you know."

"For what purpose?" asked J. Z.

"To see if he's hiding out there and not in Ireland, for one thing. So I'll need you to come with me."

"For muscle?" J. Z. raised an eyebrow.

"Well, that. We also need to hunt for clues that tie him to these crimes. And maybe the body that I saw is in there rotting under his bed." Parker shuddered.

"So, muscle and undertaker duty. Got it. But there's one problem: the roads haven't been plowed and the shuttles aren't operating. How are we going to get there?"

"We'll just have to walk."

And so began their lonely odyssey through the silent, snow-covered streets, through Harvard Square, past the **Harvard Coop**, down Plympton Street, between Quincy House on their left and the **Hillel** on their right, then past Lowell House on the right behind the Hillel. Then left onto Mill Street, down Mill past Old Leverett to De

Wolfe Street, then across De Wolfe and into the New Leverett courtyard.

"God, how long have we been walking?" panted Parker. "I don't want to be caught out here after dark with some maniac on the loose."

"Well, we got out of the diner sometime before nine A.M., and it's about, let's see . . . three thirteen now."

"Jesus, let's get going."

They walked through the courtyard to the gate on the far side, which put them out onto Cowperthwaite Street across from Dunster House, then turned left and walked down Cowperthwaite past the entrance to Dunster, finally arriving at the entrance to Mather House as the sun was slanting low over Cambridge.

They entered the lobby of Mather with their swipe cards and looked around. The house was a modern architectural maze, sculpted out of blocky concrete shapes that never quite met at right angles and stairs that spiraled upward out of the lobby to distant floors high above, sometimes ending abruptly in solid walls, as if the architect had forgotten to plan for doors. Strange, rusty sculptures cast an air of gloom amid a courtyard that never received any sunlight.

"God, it's like something out of an H. P. Lovecraft novel," commented J. Z. "I'll *literally*

Harvard mystery that's deeper and harder to solve than what goes on in the Porcellian. Maybe those people actually aren't Harvard students at all, but Lesley University students. The Harvard Coop is actually their bookstore as well, stocking the textbooks for such LU courses as Expressive Therapies, Integrated Teaching Through the Arts, and Art Therapy.

Hillel: The Jewish center, designed by world-famous architect Moshe Safdie. Great place for kosher grub and Mizmor Shir, a little Jewish a cappella.

be awake all night trying to figure this place out in my mind."

"Yeah, talk about bad feng shui. It's like if Hogwarts had been designed by Corbusier. How are we going to get into the residential areas without a resident's swipe card?"

"We'll just have to follow a resident in. People do that all the time—at least, in the other halls they do." They looked up Glenn's room number on the directory, keeping an eye to see if anyone came through the lobby.

They didn't have to wait long before a nervous-looking, slightly overweight and **pasty-faced** young man came scurrying along, hugging a stack of papers to his chest. He eyed Parker and J. Z. balefully.

pasty-faced: The concrete gloom makes all Matherites pasty-faced.

"Just hold that door open a moment, would you—hey!" exclaimed J. Z., as the kid swiped his card then leapt through the doorway, trying to slam the door on Parker and J. Z., who stuck his foot in the door at the last second. "Ow—the little creep." By the time they got through the doorway, the pasty-faced kid was nowhere to be seen.

Mercifully, they found Glenn's room without getting lost too many times, though Parker noted nervously that police or paramedics might have a very hard time locating them should the need arise.

Parker pulled a pin out of her hair and picked the simple lock in the middle of the doorknob. "Prep school trick," she whispered to J. Z. "Ready?"

She shouldered open the door, and they spilled in together.

There were no rotting bodies. After a minute, they each let out their breath, realizing no chainsaw-wielding maniac was lurking behind the door, in the closet, or suspended from the ceiling, ninja style.

What they did see was piles and piles of Celtic bric-a-brac—the odd dagger or spear here and there, but also a wide array of ancient objects of all kinds, from stylized little figurines to hammered metal jewelry, all in patterns similar to the one Parker had seen.

"Look at this," Parker said, holding up a well-worn paperback she'd taken from the desk. "Do you think it's a coincidence that the book he just happens to be reading at this particular moment is *Carmilla*?"

"Uh, you should take a look at this too, Parker." J. Z. handed her a piece of paper that he'd plucked off the bed. "Look at the header."

The header said "Barnett. *Bite Me: Le Fanu and the Lesbian Erotic Vampire Tradition*."

"It's not particularly dusty," J. Z. observed. "Not like it would be after three months in this crypt."

"That does it, J. Z. This creep is obviously stalking Neesa. We have to get back and warn her—and those nitwits at HUPD."

"I guess . . . but then I can't help thinking that we don't know too much more than we already did—Maxwell is into Irish vampire stuff. He might just have Neesa's thesis here because he was pursuing his interests."

"Well, I'm not taking any chances. My friend's in danger." Parker reflected to herself that the attack had somehow cleared up her confusion about whether she and Neesa were friends or not. Parker just wanted Neesa safe. "So do we take this stuff or leave it here?"

"Leave it—none of it's useful, but let's ask Neesa if she knew Maxwell."

* * * * *

They hurried back through the snowdrifts. Making better time than on their way there, they arrived back at Adams about fifteen minutes before **sunset**.

Parting with J. Z., who agreed to meet her for dinner later at **Quincy**, Parker went to Neesa's room without bothering to go up to her own first.

Parker opened Neesa's door and immediately noticed the musty smell of a sickroom. All of the blinds were tightly drawn, making it hard

sunset: 4:30 P.M. in winter. Should've gone to Stanford.

Quincy: Often has one of the few dining halls open during Intersession because it's located in the middle of the all the houses along the Charles River.

for Parker to make out the figure of Neesa sprawled across the bed with a pillow pressed to her head.

"Neesa, I came to see how you were. Can I get you anything?"

Neesa moaned and tossed restlessly. Parker pulled a moistened towelette from her purse (purchased to provide comfort during her flight to Barbados) and patted Neesa's brow with it, which made Neesa calm down and stop squirming.

"God, Parker, I feel like shit," said Neesa hoarsely.

"You poor thing! Just try to rest. You'll be feeling better soon. So Neesa, can I ask you a question? Do you happen to know a kid—he lives way out in Mather of all places—named Glenn Maxwell?"

Neesa didn't answer, having apparently drifted into a fitful sleep. Parker put a hand on Neesa's shoulder affectionately, and Neesa's eyelids fluttered open for a moment, fixing Parker in her stare.

"Neesa, I'm going over to Quincy soon. Do you want me to bring you back something to eat?"

At the mention of food, Neesa rolled over, stuck her head out so it wasn't over the bed, and commenced to retch.

"Oh, God. Sorry, Neesa. Just try to rest, okay? I'll check back in on you a little later." Parker stroked Neesa's hair, then, as Neesa settled back onto her bed and stared at the ceiling, glassy-eyed, she quietly left.

Parker went up the stairs to her own room to take a nap before dinner. Stepping through the doorway, she immediately sensed that something wasn't right. Then she looked at the bed.

There, on her pillow, was the stake with the Celtic design that she'd seen sticking out of the corpse's chest. It had been wiped clean, but a reddish stain had seeped into the wood.

Beside the stake was a piece of paper—or parchment. It was yellowed with age and curled into a scroll. She unfurled it and read.

Strike the maiden down before sunset,
lest she rise and stalk the night to feed.

7 Unloved Majors

Even though Harvard has fifty-one different concentrations to choose from, only a handful are actually popular. Some hardly receive any attention at all. You gotta wonder why Harvard even *has* some of the following concentrations, let alone who would devote four years to them!

Folklore and Mythology

Folk-and-Mythies are an elusive breed, so few in number that we've never even met any. Still, the concentration is worth looking into—the classes sound fluffy, the requirements look lax, and rumor has it everyone gets at least a magna on their senior thesis. Just not quite sure what you'd do with a folk and myth degree in the cold, hard, nonfiction world . . .

Statistics

Of all the unloved concentrations, stats is the most practical—grads can make a fortune for almost any company in any sector once they graduate. Money. So why doesn't anyone concentrate in it? Maybe it's too difficult. Or maybe it's because no one in the department speaks English.

Astronomy and Astrophysics

With their heads in the clouds and their butts in the far-off Harvard Observatory, these starry-eyed undergrads have nothing that resembles a normal Harvard life. Or any life, for that matter.

Near Eastern Languages and Literature

Turkish. Farsi. Hebrew. Yiddish. Rabbinic literature. Whirling dervishes. Aramaic. Rumi. Biblical archeology. Ottomans. Uzbek I. Uzbek II. Ethiopic societies. Sumerians. Akkadians. Hittites. Persian historians of past and present. And all the other things you never gave a rat's ass about.

Slavic Languages and Literature

Ack! Russian literature! Hide!

Sanskrit and Indian Studies

The number-one most unpopular concentration with the fewest undergrads matriculating every year, Sanskrit and Indian studies is basically one of those concentrations that Harvard keeps around to make the school look diverse. Honestly, how many eighteen- to twenty-one-year-olds do you know who want to concentrate in a dead language from half a world away?

Germanic Languages and Literature

Yet another "_____ languages and literature" concentration. You'd think Harvard would get a clue and scrap some of these to make room for the better, purer concentrations. *Lebensraum!*

CHAPTER
Seven

J. Z., Dunston, and Parker sat together at the nearly empty **Quincy dining hall** at dinnertime, sunk in thought.

"God, that thing was on your pillow?" J. Z. asked. "How are you ever going to sleep on that again?"

"Forget it. I'm ordering a new bed, new sheets—the works. And tonight I'm sleeping in your room. Don't get any ideas."

"It's not like I ever sleep anyway. First this crippling insomnia, now these creepy notes from the dead—"

"Ah, but to return to the issue at hand," Dunston interjected, "I think there's no doubt about what you're saying, Miss Norcross. Someone seems to be targeting Miss Barnett. And he or she seems to be suggesting that you perform some violence upon her person."

"As if! Now I'm really pissed. Neesa's my

Quincy dining hall: Built in the 1950s, Quincy dining hall feels like a ski lodge, which makes the food a tad bit more palatable. Lots of floor-to-ceiling windows provide the dining hall with plenty of natural light, unlike the dining halls in the older houses.

friend, and you should have seen her just now. She's really sick. Whoever did this is completely depraved and disgusting. And damn it, Dunston, this Glenn is not the *nice guy* you've been telling us he is. And for the last time, I'm *not* a damn slayer, so nobody say a word to me about Buffy."

"Hey, you guys! What are you all doing huddled over here, looking all serious?"

It was Neesa Barnett.

They all stared at her, open-mouthed. Neesa had put on a dark, clingy knit dress cut scandalously low. Her brown hair curled around her head in luxurious waves, and she had put on a dark red lipstick that complemented her cheeks, which were flushed as if with fever. Her eyes were unnaturally bright and piercing. She laughed at the three of them loudly.

"What's the matter with you guys? It's Intersession—we should be free to have some fun now."

Parker spoke up first. "Uh, Neesa, shouldn't you be resting? You looked pretty sick just now. What if you had fainted on the way here, out in the snow?"

"I'm fine—stop mothering me," Neesa snapped irritably. Then she brightened. "I was hoping you'd be here, Parker. All of you. I think you all should come by my room for a party tonight. Yes, you too, Dunston. I really don't feel like being alone tonight."

"Well, that's understandable," said Parker. "Yes, let's hang out. J. Z. can bring the booze, right, J. Z.?" J. Z. nodded, cautiously.

"Are you going to eat anything, Neesa?" Parker asked.

"We're pretty much done, but we'd be happy to stay with you while you eat."

"Oh, no, not much appetite. You guys should go. I'll see you a bit later, in my room—right, guys?" Then, as they were leaving, Neesa slipped her arm under Parker's and pulled Parker toward her so that Parker's body was almost pressed up against hers. Parker could feel how hot Neesa was through their clothes. "Stay back and walk with me, Parker. I want to talk with you."

Parker nodded, letting Neesa hold her back, though she felt a little uncomfortable about it.

"Parker, don't leave me alone tonight. I don't want to be alone." Her voice was urgent.

"Uh, yeah, okay, Neesa. I totally understand. You can stay with me. Let me get my bag and we can go to my—" She paused, thinking about not wanting to go back into her room. But the scroll and stake were in her bag, and she really had nowhere else to go. She was thankful she didn't have to go back to it alone. In fact, she realized she wanted company as much as Neesa did.

* * * * *

Back in Parker's room, Neesa sat back on the bed, stretching her legs out and eying Parker languidly. Parker fiddled with the thermostat, feeling a sudden chill. Neesa smiled at her, her full ruby-colored lips glossy and wet. She patted the bed, signaling for Parker to come sit by her. Parker did sit down but tried to keep a slight distance between herself and Neesa. Then, feeling squirmy and uncomfortable, she leapt up suddenly.

"Do you want a glass of wine or something, Neesa?" Parker was unsure what to do with herself. Neesa nodded, smiling.

Parker took a bottle of wine from under her bed, scrounged around for an opener, pulled a wineglass from her bookshelf, then, noticing it was dusty, went into the **bathroom** and started to rinse it out in the sink. The glass slipped out of her hand, shattering on the metal stopper. Parker realized her hands were shaking. She reached down to pluck the shards from the sink and cut her hand. Blood dripped into the bowl of the sink.

Suddenly, Neesa was in the bathroom doorway. "Oh, you poor thing, let me help you!"

Parker whirled around to face her, clutching her cut finger to her chest protectively, her heart beating like mad. Neesa calmly opened the medicine cabinet, took out a gauze pad and some tape, and reached out tentatively toward Parker.

Parker slowly, hesitantly unfolded her arm and let Neesa take it. Neesa ran Parker's hand under tepid water, patted it dry with the gauze, and wrapped it up with tape. At Neesa's gentle, competent touch, Parker could feel chills

bathroom: All dorm rooms in the upper-class houses have their own bathrooms *en suite*. Sounds pretty swank compared to state schools, but not as posh as the select few kids whose rooms come with kitchens too!

running up her arm and down her spine. Neesa patted her hand lightly and smiled.

"There, all better."

Parker smiled back, waiting for Neesa to release her hand.

Then, suddenly but not forcefully, Neesa pulled on Parker's arm, drawing Parker toward her for a kiss. Mesmerized, Parker didn't pull back. Neesa's lips clamped over hers, and Neesa's arms wrapped around Parker's neck, her fingers twining in Parker's ash blond hair.

The Houses
of Harvard

Sophomores, juniors, and seniors live in one of thirteen upper-class dorms, called houses. Houses range in size from roughly 300 to 900 students, but all have the same basic features: a dining hall, a library, common rooms, meeting rooms, music practice rooms, weight rooms, and, of course, dorm rooms. Each house has its own distinct personality, much of which carries over from the days when students were allowed to choose their own house. Even though the university randomized house assignments in the mid 1990s, first-years are still allowed to form blocking groups of up to eight freshmen who will be randomly assigned as a group to a house at the end of their freshman year. Nine of the houses are along the Charles River, three are in the Radcliffe Quadrangle, and one is in Harvard Yard.

Adams House

River. Adamsites like to think they're all that and a slice of quiche, but they're only special because they live closest to Harvard Yard at the center of campus. Once the posh home of Harvard's wealthiest, artsy Adams opened its doors to the rank and file in 1996, undoubtedly causing namesakes John and John Quincy to roll in their graves. Famous for its swimming-pool-o'-orgies (sadly, now drained), psychedelic underground passageways, Drag Night and Masquerade, and black-tie readings of Winnie the Pooh.

Cabot House

Quad. Although Cabot House physically dominates the Quad with its six expansive brick buildings, it has always played second fiddle to its spunkier neighbors Currier and PfoHo. Hmm, sounds a lot like Canada, actually: big, lumbering, yet forgotten. And much like those crazy Canucks, any Cabotian will tell you how unique Cabot is with its unrivaled house spirit (*uh-huh*), milk-and-cookie study breaks (*okaay*), and annual tutor performance of the *Grinch Who Stole Christmas* (*riiiiiiiight*). Just nod yes and maybe they'll go away.

Currier House

Quad. A former hotel, Currier is now the smallest house, with just under 300 people. Truly a maze of doorways, stairways, hallways, and passageways, you'll be lucky to ever retrace your steps without using a ball of string. The large foyers downstairs make up for the cramped, single rooms upstairs, but the spacious dining hall's fountain and chill atmosphere make Currier one of the best places to enjoy a leisurely meal with friends— if you can drag your ass out there, that is.

Dunster House

River. If you've seen a picture of Harvard, you've seen Dunster. Postcard photographers love its picturesque dome and prime real estate along the Charles. On the other hand, the rooms are tiny, the entrance is smelly, and Al Gore once lived there, reinforcing the ABC-special axiom that you can't judge a book by its cover—or a dorm by its dome. The annual goat roast, moreover, is hilarious, but disgusting. No wonder everyone calls it Dumpster House.

Eliot House

River. Ah, Eliot. Where the men row boats and the women eat ivy. As the flagship house, Eliot embodies all things Harvard, with its beauty, charm, and fancy parties. The sense of elitist cliquishness—er . . . community—and the irresistibly sexy Italian house master, Lino, make up for the cramped quarters and serious overcrowding. Skip the Evening with Champions figure skating gala (lame), but be sure to finagle an invite to the Spring Fete formal (positively smashing). *Caviar, darling?*

Kirkland House

River. Small and tucked away, Kirkland House has friendly, studious people and arguably the best Sunday brunch. The winter holidays get a little crazy, with raucous Secret Santa pranks, roast pig parades, kazoo concerts, and the annual IncestFest, when everyone gets freaky with their neighbors. Don't let the security guard scare you—he may be a smart ass, but his tough exterior belies a mushy teddy bear heart of gold. *Awwww!* And he can tell you the day of the week you were born if you tell him your b-day. Superfreaky.

Leverett House

River. The classic red brick façade of this Harvard house almost dupes you into forgetting that most of its residents live in the butt-ugly towers across the street. Almost. Students also have to put up with the god-awful painting that hangs in the dining hall because no other house can accommodate such large banquets and club parties. Still, there's something friendly and appealing about the place. You just can't hate a house with cute little bunny rabbits for mascots.

Lowell House

River. Any dorm crewer will tell you that there're more roaches in Lowell than in all the other houses combined—and we don't mean the students. A favorite campus tour stop, the picture-perfect double courtyard and grandiose bell tower add flavor to this otherwise dull house. It's big, it's brick, and it bites.

Mather House

River. Better known as the box that Dunster came in, this gloomy concrete fortress with the phallic corner tower stands guard on the Charles next to Dumpster. More than one freshman has screamed in horror upon being sentenced to this real-world Azkaban. Yet Mather eventually wins the heart of every resident with its guaranteed singles, a spectacular eighteen-story tower view, and the soapy-sudsy-sketchy Mather Lather dance. House motto: Bigger *Is* Better.

Pforzheimer House

Quad. After the initial gnashing of teeth and beating of breasts that accompany banishment to the Quad, freshmen soon discover that small Pforzheimer House, or PfoHo, actually has a lot to offer. Plenty of house spirit, spacious suites, and a unique dining hall make life as a Quadling enjoyable, despite the fact that you'll need a map to get there and another to find your way around. *PfoHo, MoFo!*

Quincy House

River. Harvard spawned this Frankenstein monster of a house after building state-school concrete-block housing next to Leverett's neo-Georgian annex, rechristening the entire conglomeration Quincy House. *Whew!* What a mouthful. Still, the unholy mishmash of architectural styles somehow works well. The cubic Qube library (*Get it?! Get it?!*) is quite quool (*Get it?!*), as is the student-run grill that's open late nights on the weekends.

Winthrop House

River. With its two buildings, three courtyards, and numerous trees and statues, Winthrop House sprawls alongside the Charles on prime Cambridge real estate. Even though Winthrop has the worst housing on campus, Winthropians are nevertheless a friendly and sociable bunch who're always up for a good time.

Dudley House

Yard. Not quite a house, not quite a student union, Dudley House is where the few students who live off campus congregate to whine about how hard it is to live off campus. No house pride, no house spirit, no one cares.

Frosh Dorms

All first-years must live in the freshman dorms, most of which are located in Harvard Yard in the middle of campus. Freshman deans assign students to rooms prior to the move-in date and try hard to make good roommate matches based on the information in students' applications, intense personality profiles, polygraph tests, and reaction to Chinese water torture.

Hollis

Large and luxurious single-room doubles means you'll be bunking in style—or dividing the room with flimsy Japanese screens trying to convince yourself you have some semblance of privacy. Famous frosh: Ralph Waldo Emerson, Henry David Thoreau, John Updike.

Stoughton

Filled with more studio-size doubles, living in Stoughton means living it up state-school style, despite the ancient brick façade. Outshined by neighbors Hollis and Holworthy at the north end of the Yard, you'll probably never really notice Stoughton unless you actually live there. Famous frosh: Edward Zwick, John Berendt.

Grays

Spacious yet quaint, Grays stands guard over the south end of the Yard. Quads with enormous common rooms make Grays a great place to kick back with friends, maybe even a famous one living in the Grays Middle celebrity suite. Famous frosh: Natalie Portman, Mo Rocca, Ryan Fitzpatrick.

Holworthy

Opposite Grays at the north end of the Yard, Holworthy also features sociable quads with large common rooms. Famous frosh: Conan O'Brien, Howard Hughes, Henry Adams.

Weld

The big daddy of them all, Weld is only one of two frosh dorms with hallways instead of entryways. Enormous suites also mean you don't have to procrastinate alone, especially with that kickass glass-ceiling common room on the top floor. Famous frosh: John F. Kennedy, Tatyana Ali, Michael Crichton.

Thayer

Most convenient to the food and large lecture halls—everything a freshman needs. Long hallways make meeting people easy. Now if it weren't for those damn church bells next door or the Victorian ghosts that supposedly haunt the hallways. Famous frosh: E. E. Cummings, Jonathan Taylor Thomas, James Agee, Steve Ballmer.

Lionel

Tucked away behind Hollis, Harvard Hall, and Holden Chapel, tiny Lionel is a great place to live if you value your privacy or need to hide from the cops. Famous frosh: Lou Dobbs.

Mower

Small, with only thirty people, Mower is known for its strong dorm pride and incestuous entryways. Kitchen and common room with cable in the basement. *Mower Power!* Famous frosh: Al Gore and Tommy Lee Jones (roomies!), Al Franken.

Wigglesworth

The longest dorm, Wigg stretches the entire width of the Yard. It's so long that people in Wigg A may never even meet their homeys in Wigg J. Large suites and a basement pool table compensate for the traffic noise on Mass Ave. Famous frosh: Bill Gates, Ted Kennedy, John Lithgow, Robert Lowell.

Pennypacker

Centrally located decades ago near the now-destroyed student union, Pennypacker is now the frosh dorm farthest from Harvard Yard. Four floors of quads and quints all built around an open, central stairwell make the Pack just as famous for parties as some of the upper-class houses. Famous frosh: Nicholas D. Kristof.

Greenough

Another union dorm far far away, Greenough is filled with psycho-single rooms so small you have to climb over your dresser to get to your bed. Old, isolated, and quite possibly the worst freshman dorm. Hook up with someone in the Yard so you'll never have to walk home. Famous frosh: Wallace Shawn.

Hurlbut

The third and smallest of the union dorms, Hurlbut consists of students in singles that no one ever seems to visit. Also home to many orthodox Jews, who enter through traditional lock-and-key doors without using an electronic swipe card on the Sabbath. And the obvious butt (pun intended) of many lame freshmen jokes. Famous frosh: James Blake.

Apley Court

Former apartments in the middle of Harvard Square. Traditionally known for tight-knit entryways that isolate themselves from other freshmen. A fun place where, rumor has it, anything can happen. Famous frosh: T. S. Eliot

Matthews

Brick gothic architecture with large entryways and spacious suites makes this Yard icon truly unique. Five floors, no elevators—sucks to be you. Famous frosh: Matt Damon, William Randolph Hearst, Michael Chertoff, John Dos Passos.

Massachusetts Hall

One of the oldest buildings on campus, Mass Hall not only houses twenty or so of the best, brightest, and quietest freshmen, but also the offices of the university's president. *Ew.* Famous frosh: Samuel Adams, John Adams, John Hancock.

Canaday

The newest frosh dorm, Canaday's functional architecture is rumored to be riot proof with its small windows and narrow stairwells, just in case students revolt again like they did in 1969. Too bad, though there are plenty of other dorms to raise a ruckus in. Famous frosh: Paul Wylie, Mira Sorvino.

Straus

Wedged between Mass Ave. and Mass Hall, Straus always seems to get lost in the shuffle. It has a great first floor common room, though, that's just perfect for all those boring, mandatory entryway meetings you never wanted to attend. Famous frosh: William S. Burroughs, Soledad O'Brian, Darren Aronofsky.

CHAPTER
Eight

"Jesus, J. Z., open up already."

J. Z. opened his door to find Parker outside, visibly agitated, her face flushed. "What's the matter, Parker? You weren't attacked, were you?"

"Not exactly, no."

"What the hell does that mean? Are you okay?"

"Jesus," Parker panted. "Just give me something, would you? I'm not ready for questions."

J. Z. turned and walked back into his room, taking a bottle down from his bookshelf. He poured some out into a glass and offered it to Parker.

Parker took it and gulped it down. A searing heat lit up the inside of her mouth, making her eyes water. Gradually, the fire subsided, and a warm glow permeated her body. She looked at J. Z. gratefully.

"What on earth *was* that, J. Z.?"

"Tsipouro. It's distilled from the must left over in a grape press. Monks in Macedonia make it." He sat down and looked at Parker, who still said nothing. "What's gotten into you?"

"Just been a long day."

"Where's Neesa? I thought she wanted to hang with you?"

"She does . . . she did . . . we did," Parker stammered.

J. Z. raised his eyebrows quizzically, waiting for more. Then, when more was not forthcoming, "You agree there's something not right about her, don't you?"

"I don't know . . . what do you mean?"

"Well, she's sick one moment and then bouncing off the walls the next. She didn't seem like she was acting, I don't know, a little *strange* when she came by at dinner? A little intense?"

"She's always intense. I was glad to see her, I don't know . . . up and around."

"Up and around. Up and around . . . hmm. I guess that's one way to describe it. So you didn't find anything out from her when you two went off together?"

Well, I found out one thing, Parker thought to herself. *She's a pretty good kisser. . .*

"There's something that doesn't add up about all this," said J. Z., "but I haven't put my finger on what it is."

Parker could tell from the look on his face that he was determined to put his finger on it come hell or high water, and the thought made her squirm. In an effort to get his formidable brain moving in a different direction, she ventured, "Um, J. Z., maybe the attack has something to do with Neesa's thesis. We did find that page in Glenn Maxwell's room, after all. You've read *Carmilla*—what's the story with it?"

"Oh, that, yes. Well, it's a pretty good read, actually. Shorter than *Dracula*, and fewer characters and subplots. It's narrated by a young woman. Her earliest memory is that, when she was about six, she was visited at night, in her nursery, by a beautiful young woman who bit her on the breast—though she was told by her father that this must have been a dream. Later, when she's grown up, she meets a girl named Carmilla, who comes to stay with her at her family's castle. She recognizes Carmilla as the woman in her dream, but Carmilla claims to have had an identical dream in which she was bitten by the narrator. Anyway, the two become friends, and Carmilla starts making these erotic advances on the narrator—hugging her, kissing her, acting sort of wild, and making impetuous declarations of love. The narrator says this embarrasses her, but you can tell by how she acts that she kind of likes it."

Parker flushed at this, but she was glad to have gotten him onto the subject of literature, his forte.

"Anyway, she dreams again that she's been bitten on the breast, but this time it's by a giant cat, which is presumably one of Carmilla's forms. The narrator and her father eventually figure out Carmilla's a vampire and kill her. I know what you're thinking—no, not with a stake. They dig up her body and cut her head off, if I recall correctly."

* * * * *

Now, this was the J. Z. that Parker was familiar with—lucid mind, sharp wit, tireless intellectual curiosity. Parker's mind

**Bureau of Study
Council:** Not to be
confused with teen
series *The Babysitters'
Club*, Harvard's BSC
offers advice and tutors
for students who need
a little extra help. On
second thought, all that
extra handholding and
encouragement really
does make it seem like
the Babysitters' Club.
The BSC also offers
courses and seminars
on how to pass your,
um, other courses
and seminars. Yeah,
like stressed-out kids
who're barely passing
their classes are going
to sign up for any more.
Panicked students
would be wise to hire
a BSC tutor—another
undergrad who's
survived your course
and will coach you to
success.

"failing" grade (B):
Students everywhere—
but particularly Harvard
students—like to bitch
and moan a lot about
their grades. For many
students, getting
anything below a B+
or an A– does feel like
failing. Whiny little
prats—you know you'll
be making a fortune a
few years after you're
out anyway no matter
how poorly you do!

went back to her first meeting with J. Z. during her sophomore year, when, being in danger of "failing" (i.e., getting a B in an English seminar on Nabokov), she had gone to the **Bureau of Study Council** to find herself an English tutor.

"Oh, I think you'll be pleased with J. Z." winked Julie, the receptionist. "He's as smart as they get and not bad to look at either."

Parker had been too concerned with her grades at the time to even consider romance a possibility. Though that wasn't to say that she wasn't totally floored by J. Z. the moment she met him. But it wasn't his blue eyes, tousled brown hair, or goofy, lopsided grin that did her in (although Parker admittedly was seeing more and more to like about J. Z. in the past twenty-four hours); it was his razor sharp intellect. Right away, Parker could tell that she would have to work twice as hard as before to even keep up with him. Although she had already read Nabokov's *Pale Fire* from cover to cover before their first meeting, she hadn't picked up on half of the subtle nuances that J. Z. pulled from the text. He pushed her to think about literature from all angles, and while Parker had to train herself to work that way, it seemed like a sort of second sense to J. Z. With a semester of excellent coaching, Parker was able to raise her **"failing" grade (B)** to a satisfactory one (A–) and made a worthy and reliable friend in the process.

Parker stared pensively at the ground for a few seconds. The kiss with Neesa had thrown her completely off her stride. Deprived of any time for reflection, she hadn't even realized she'd been developing feelings for J. Z. until she realized she didn't want to tell him about the kiss with Neesa—which she wasn't even sure *how* to feel about. Though it was electrifying, no question.

"Look, Parker, here's what's not right here. All day we've been saying the attacks must have been by this crazy Glenn Maxwell from Mather. The lone-maniac theory seems to have a lot going for it: it doesn't require us to believe in vampires; it keeps things simple, since there's only one guy doing the attacking; and he does live in Mather, after all."

"But . . . ?"

"But it doesn't explain why Neesa is acting the way she is. She's acting like she actually *was* bitten by a vampire, so either she's working with this maniac—which would imply that he's not actually crazy, by the way—or . . . I don't know."

"Or she actually *was* bitten by a vampire," Parker finished. "You're right—what if instead of going crazy, Glenn Maxwell actually went to Ireland and found this Abhartach, and Abhartach bit him and sent him back to Harvard as a vampire? Or what if Abhartach **came to Harvard himself**?"

came to Harvard himself: Wow, he got in. Great grades, activities, and a killer essay can do that for you.

"Oh, please, Parker, let's not get carried away."

"Well, you're the one who brought it up."

"All I said was that her behavior didn't add up."

"Well, how are we supposed to know if Neesa was really bitten? What are the signs?"

"Well, I'm no Glenn Maxwell, but . . . in most of the books, the person who is bitten—who's usually called the *thrall*—is sick during the day then better at night, seems sexually voracious and preternaturally attractive—only at night, of course. And you can't reason with them. They're secretly *always* thinking about the 'master' who bit them, and they'll always outwit every attempt to keep them in bed and protected. They *want* to go to their master, and they're happy to seduce others and lead them to destruction while they're doing it."

J. Z. paused for a moment to reflect, then continued. "So, basically the only real oddity about Neesa is that she started feeling better at sundown."

"She didn't seem, uh, how did you put it—'preternaturally attractive'?"

"Well, she's kind of hot, I guess, though she's plenty pretentious too. But no—she seemed more or less like Neesa to me. Why do you ask?" J. Z. looked at Parker sharply.

"Well, I, uh . . . J. Z., I kissed her. Or she kissed me. Or something."

"You *WHAT*?!" J. Z. spluttered. "Do you realize how dangerous that could be?"

"But you just got through telling me how she wasn't a

thrall. You're just jealous."

"I am *not* jealous! God, you're making me crazy. I'm going to be up all night reliving this idiotic experience. I'm just saying she's dangerous, is all."

"Look, either you believe she's a thrall or you don't. After all, maybe it was just her spooky thrall powers that got to me," she offered, trying to toss him a bone.

"Maybe." J. Z. glared at her. "You know, if she is a thrall, we ought to be trying to protect her from further attack," he said, his mouth dry.

"You said yourself that never works."

"Then I suppose . . . one of us might have to kill her." J. Z. eyed her narrowly, waiting to see what she said.

Parker glared back at him defiantly. "Forget it, J. Z. I'm half convinced, but I'm not *that* convinced. And I think . . . I think I may have feelings for her."

"Terrific. Look, you know, I think I'm going to take a little walk. I don't really feel like going to Neesa's 'party' tonight."

"Fine."

"Fine." He stalked out, muttering.

Harvard Hookups

5 Types of Relationships That Are Better Avoided

Studious and highly stressed, Harvard students forgo normality and break all the relationship rules that exist for good reasons.

TF/Tutor Tango

Innocent, doe-eyed girl ditches her "immature" male classmates to be with her tweed-clad house tutor or teaching fellow. Passionate but brief, and fizzles out in a month when rumors of pedophilia spread. Lo. Lee. Ta.

Frosh Week Marriage

A small but surprising number of Freshman Week hookups last for what seems like a lifetime. For better or worse. Richer or poorer. Till death—or graduation—do them part. Disgusting. Sickening.

Primal Scream Voyeurism

No matter the weather, Harvard undergrads gather at midnight before the first day of finals to get nekkid and run screaming around the Yard. Many run, even more watch, and more than a few fall in love.

Quad/River Relationship

Even though long distance kills most Quad/River relationships before they really heat up, you may see a few frumpy students making the so-called walk of shame back home along Garden or Brattle Streets early in the morning. Yep, everyone knows you got down and dirty last night and are apparently regretting it this morning.

Blockcest

First and only rule when forming a blocking group: BFF B4 BF/GF. Frosh love flickers but briefly and it'd suck to be stuck next to your ex for three *looong* years.

CHAPTER
Nine

Parker was walking through a prehistoric forest shrouded in thick mist. She was wearing a white robe of rough wool, a druidess's robe, which dragged across the pine needles on the ground as she strode out of the woods and into a kind of clearing or grove. The grove was bounded by trees with silver-colored bark that Parker thought might be ash trees. In the center of the clearing was a large black cauldron filled with what looked to Parker like mussels or oysters, pulled from the shores of the North Atlantic.

Two figures strode into the clearing from different sides, both robed in white just like Parker. One was J. Z., but he had a long beard and wore a strange, Celtic-looking metal band around his neck. In his hand was a silver chalice, which he held out to Parker, smiling. Parker took the chalice from him, looking into his gentle gray eyes.

Suddenly, the forests echoed with cold, brittle laughter, as if from an old and very evil man whom Parker could not see and whose location she could not even begin to guess. She turned to look at the second white-robed figure, who now stood

on the other side of the cauldron, resting her hands on its rim invitingly and smiling across it at Parker.

It was Neesa Barnett.

As if compelled by an irresistible force, Parker glided toward her through the Celtic mists until she stood over the cauldron. She looked down at the black mussels inside, then reached down to pick one up.

The mussel sprang open at her touch, and her fingers sunk deep into the slimy, gelatinous flesh, which felt warm and yielding.

Parker cried out as a sharp pain sliced through her finger amid the warm moistness. The mussel shell had cut into her finger like a razor blade. The sensation of moist slipperiness swelled up her fingers past her knuckles, lapping at the space between each finger, as the blood oozed out into the flesh of the mussel. Her finger began to throb, and the pain increased.

Parker woke up, but neither the throbbing nor the warm, moist sensation faded.

Neesa Barnett was crouched beside the bed, sucking the blood out of Parker's cut finger.

Join Up!

13 Colorful Clubs

The Krokodiloes

Suave, sophisticated, and slightly raunchy, the all-male Harvard Krokodiloes a cappella group is a Harvard institution in and of itself. Hands down the coolest guys on campus, Krok crooners can bag any girl they like when not performing for kings, queens, and crowds around the world. Greatest hit singles: "Danny Boy," "Loch Lomond," "10,000 Men of Harvard," and "The Masochism Tango."

The Porcellian

Located on Mass Ave. next to a crappy Chinese restaurant, The Porcellian is Harvard's most elite all-male Final Club—a quasi secret society. Rumor has it that members are guaranteed to make at least a million dollars a year for the rest of their lives. Only made six figures your first year out? No worries, The Porc's got you covered. Then again, you have to wonder about a bunch of college guys who still won't let girls play in their clubhouse.

The Harvard *Lampoon*

Founded in 1876, Harvard's premier comic rag, the Harvard *Lampoon*, is based in the so-called Lampoon Castle on Mt. Auburn Street, a building donated by William Randolph Hearst himself and purportedly a veritable playpen filled with all things fun.

The Hasty Pudding

Founded in 1795, the Hasty Pudding is not only the nation's oldest theatrical society but probably America's oldest drag show as well. Clever and comedic with no pretensions of seriousness, the Pudding's shows draw thousands every year. Though you may be too broke to ever see a show, check out the free annual Man/Woman of the Year parades when the Pudding honors Hollywood's finest—in drag, of course.

The *Crimson*

With so much always happening, newsmakers and muckrakers alike get their start at the Harvard *Crimson*, America's second-oldest daily college newspaper (Yalies had the first, those rat bastards). As an aspiring frosh reporter, you may get your feet wet and hands dirty covering the latest scandal, interviewing visiting dignitaries, or (more likely) stuffing envelopes in the mail room.

The Crimson Key

The closest thing Harvard has to a pep squad, the red-shirted Crimson Keyers are always on hand to . . . to . . . do . . . something important, we're sure. These meeters and greeters are highly visible (and annoying) during Freshman Week with their "Let's go!" spirit and parent-friendly smiles. Then they disappear until it's time to suck up to alums during reunions in May.

Phillips Brooks House Association

PBHA is Harvard's umbrella organization that oversees dozens of community service projects in Cambridge and Boston. More than two-thirds of all undergrads volunteer in a PBHA program at some point during their four years. Check out Chinatown ESL and Chinatown Afterschool, Mission Hill Afterschool, Boston Refugee Youth Enrichment, Keylatch, and the Legal Committee, among others.

Undergraduate Council

Harvard undergrads' student council, the UC, might as well just not exist. Honestly, how much power do you think students have at a nearly 400-year-old institution run by a bunch of secretive old farts? Still, the UC presidency is a coveted position among the nation's young generation of movers and shakers.

Harvard Student Agencies

Any enterprising young Harvardian should try his or her hand at HSA, Harvard's organization for . . . um, enterprising young Harvardians. Supposedly the largest student-run corporation in the world, HSA dabbles in publishing, marketing, translation, and even cleaning. Or you can enroll in the popular bartending course to learn all about the drinks your degree guarantees you'll never have to pour for anyone else.

Let's Go

An offshoot of HSA, *Let's Go* publishes an award-winning series of student travel guides written and edited entirely by Harvard kids. Never mind they've been steadily declining in popularity since those flashy *Lonely Planets* hit the market. Still, how many other kids do you know who've been published at twenty and can say they got paid to backpack India for a summer?

Institute of Politics

The IOP is *the* place to be if you're a gov jock, a social studies concentrator, or simply like current affairs. Write for the Harvard *Political Review*, take seminars on speech writing, organize conferences, and help get out the vote. Or just use your free time to hobnob with prime ministers, presidents, and parliamentarians.

CityStep

A vivacious bunch, CityStep volunteers dedicate themselves to improving and enriching the lives of Boston's inner-city youth through dance. Though we never quite figured out exactly how dancing prevents violence, substance abuse, and teen pregnancy, the program is nevertheless wildly popular on campus and in the neighborhoods it serves. *Oooo! Aaah! CityStep, CityStep, CityStep, CityStep!*

Radcliffe Pitches

The Radcliffe Bitches—oops, *P*itches!—is Harvard's all-female a cappella group. Somehow, though, they just don't sound as good as the all-male Kroks. You'll undoubtedly have to sit through the Bitches'—oops, *P*itches'!— mini teaser concerts at the end of large lecture classes.

Ten

Parker leaped up onto her feet on top of the bed, backing herself up against the wall as if she'd seen a rat.

Neesa recoiled as well, skittering backward on all fours and hissing at Parker, her eyes flashing. She looked as if she were about to pounce.

The two stared at each other for a moment, panting.

Then, slowly, Parker's bag, which had been propped open at the foot of the bed, toppled over, spilling its contents onto the floor. The stake fell onto the wood floor with a loud clatter. Parker's eyes met Neesa's briefly from across the room. Then Parker lunged for the stake as Neesa dove at her, hissing.

Parker managed to get her fingers on the stake just as Neesa collided with her, knocking her back into the side of the bed. The two of them rolled over each other, clawing for control of the stake. Neesa grabbed the neck of Parker's ivory silk turtleneck and yanked, ripping the fabric.

Parker put her palm in the middle of Neesa's chest and pushed with all her weight, grunting. Neesa fell onto the floor, and Parker raised the stake above her head, taking aim at

Neesa's heart. She brought the stake down, putting all of her weight into it.

Suddenly, Neesa rolled out of the way, and the stake glanced across her ribs, tearing her dress and nailing a scrap of it to the floor of J. Z.'s room. Neesa leapt up, clutching her torn dress to herself, her black lace bra showing.

Neesa hissed at Parker from the doorway. "You think you've escaped, but the master will deal with you!" Then she slipped through the doorway and fled, her black dress flying behind her.

Parker was still gasping for air and looking in horror at the stake nailed to the floor when a very flustered Gigi Cross came into her room.

"Gigi, I can explain—"

"Explain what? Parker—you have to come outside." Gigi, too, was gasping for breath. "You were right—the police just found a dead body in front of **Widener**, buried in the snow. You have to come. Now."

Widener: Short for Widener Library. The snow-covered front steps are a great place to go sledding, by the way.

* * * * *

Parker's heart pounded loudly in her chest as she sprinted down the stairs of Adams House and into the lobby. She pushed open the doors of A-entryway and began to run toward the Yard.

The snow clung to her shoes in clumps as she awkwardly skidded her way up **Bow Street**. Even though the plows had finally made their rounds through the streets, the snow was still piled high along the sides of the road, and what remained was packed into a dense ice that was dangerously slippery to run on.

Out of the corner of her eye, Parker noticed packs of other upperclassmen stragglers who were making their way to the Yard to see what all the fuss was about. Parker could only think about the dead body: was it, in fact, the body that she had seen the night before, or had the killer struck again?

Parker trotted across the street and entered into the Yard through the **Class of 1875 gate**. As she passed through it, she saw the **veritas** shield, Harvard's emblematic motto, poised at the top, along with the inscription, "**Open ye the gates** that the righteous nation which keepeth the truth may enter in." Truth had taken on a completely different meaning to Parker since she had been snowed in by the storm. It seemed like no one was able to see or understand all of it; even Parker, who had seen everything firsthand, could not wrap her mind around the bigger picture, the grander scheme. Parker knew that she would find the truth tonight. Her thoughts turned

Bow Street: One of the little side streets connecting Mass Ave. to Mt. Auburn Street, intersected by (surprise!) Arrow Street. Former site of the hip little Bow and Arrow Pub (now closed) made famous in *Good Will Hunting.*

Class of 1875 gate: Anyone entering the Yard must pass through one of several wrought-iron gates, most of which were donated by various graduating classes over the past two centuries. The main entrance to the Yard is Johnston Gate, located on the west side of Harvard Yard and featured on dozens of postcards. Superstition has it that undergrads may walk through Johnston Gate only on their first and last days at Harvard and will fail or drop out if they pass through it any other time.

veritas: Latin for "truth."

Open ye the gates . . . : Dante would've been more accurate— "Abandon hope all ye who enter here."

momentarily toward J. Z.

I wish I had him with me now, she thought regretfully. *Will we ever be friends again?*

But it was too late to turn back now. After slipping through the gate, Parker looked up at the looming back wall of Widener Library. As she rounded the front of the building, Parker saw several HUPD police cars scattered across the Yard, their red lights flashing and engines still running. A section of ground to the right of the front staircase of the library was roped off with police tape. Police were swarming all over the area with flashlights; two had guns. A large crowd of freshman and upperclassmen had gathered just outside of the crime scene, huddled together and shivering.

Parker saw her old friends, Officers Nikita and Sanchez, standing in the center of the other officers. There was no joking around anymore. As soon as they saw her enter the Yard, they motioned for her to come over. With a heavy heart, Parker walked up to the two officers and peeked over the roped-off area of the crime scene. What she saw made her stomach turn. It was the same body. The flashing lights of the cop cars and the pale yellow glow of the library lights cast themselves on the body, sprawled out across the bottom steps of the library in a pile of snow. The body looked just as it had before, except that his exposed flesh had a bluish tinge to it that gave the scene an even eerier effect. Parker shielded her eyes and looked away.

"Miss Norcross, is this the body you saw? The body that you initially reported to us last night?" asked Officer Nikita.

"Yes officer, it is."

"Look," said Officer Sanchez, "when we came over, we had no idea you were serious."

"Miss Norcross. This has turned into a homicide investigation. The Cambridge police will be arriving shortly. You realize you're our primary witness."

"Yes."

"Now, just stay right here and wait until they come."

"Sure."

As the stunned HUPD officers left her side to consult with their peers, Parker noticed Dunston Peck standing alone on the stage of Memorial Church across the length of the Yard. Parker squinted to get a better look. He was wringing his hands nervously and pacing back and forth. Parker glanced around, saw that the officers weren't looking, and slipped over to him. When Dunston spotted Parker walking up the steps, he dropped his hands to his sides and sighed.

"Dunston?" Parker asked. "Hey, what's wrong?" She stopped herself. She knew already what was wrong.

Dunston wasn't listening anyway. He continued to pace nervously and wring his hands.

"Sweet Mary's milk!" whispered Dunston, his voice choked with grief. "That's Glenn Maxwell!" Parker put a hand on Dunston's shoulder to comfort him, trying to think of a reason why someone would want to kill this poor young man.

"There she is, officers! There's the girl who just tried to attack me!"

A shrill, hysterical voice pierced through the air. Parker's head whipped around with a start, and she could see a very frantic Neesa Barnett dragging the weary-looking HUPD officers across the Yard in her direction.

Oh no, Parker thought. *What the hell is she doing now? Is she going to attack those cops? Is she going to come after me again? Is her "master" here somewhere?*

Parker straightened her back to face Neesa, her fists clenched, bracing herself for violence.

"Officers, don't let her near me!" shrieked Neesa, "She's crazed. She just tried to stab me with a stake two minutes ago! I think she must be on PCP or something. The stake is either in her pocket or in her boyfriend's room—it must have her fingerprints all over it." She paused, panting. "I wouldn't be surprised if that was your murder weapon too."

Parker froze. *No way, you bitch*, she thought. In her rush to get to the Yard, she had left the stake stuck in the floor and ran out the door. This was bad. Very bad.

"Look, I can explain . . ."

Officer Sanchez's eyes widened.

"Do you mean to tell me this girl is *serious*? You have a *stake* in your room?"

"Well, J. Z.'s room now, but it was planted on my bed and . . . and . . . Neesa came into my room and started sucking on my finger, and—"

Officers Nikita and Sanchez shared a knowing look. A look that said clearly, *She's nuts.* They turned to Parker.

"So, all this time you were right under our noses, eh?" said Officer Nikita. "Nice try with the claiming-to-find-the-body routine. All this time you seemed so sane and reasonable. It goes to show you never can tell."

Parker felt hot tears welling up in her eyes. She glared at Neesa, who had a giant smirk plastered across her face. Parker pointed a trembling finger in Neesa's direction.

"It's her fault! She's setting me up! I swear I'm telling you the truth—I didn't do anything!" Parker cried.

Neesa ripped the Band-Aid off her neck to expose her still-raw puncture wounds.

"Isn't it obvious?" Neesa shrieked, pointing to her neck. "She did this! She did it all! She's obsessed with me—and jealous of my senior thesis. She's been reading the same books trying to rival me—and now she's snapped."

Parker rolled her eyes at this.

"But officers, please don't be too hard on her. It's not really her fault—it's this *school*. Some people just can't take the hyper-competitive atmosphere. Every year someone cracks—if not more than one. I mean, come on," she said, starting to wax eloquent in her triumph, "don't you feel just a little sorry for a girl who gets so obsessed with some old French story about some lesbian vampires that she actually thinks *she's* a lesbian vampire? I know I do. Gender theory helps me keep a healthy perspective on *literature*" (in pronouncing the word, she allowed a hint of disdain to creep into her voice) "by keeping it politically and socially relevant."

Dunston started to slowly back away from Parker.

"Is this true, Miss Norcross?" he said, trembling. "Is what Miss Barnett is saying . . . *true*?"

"I'm inclined to believe the girl who's been attacked," said

Officer Sanchez to Dunston.

Neesa continued. "Really, I think what's going on is that Parker uses the persona of Carmilla to act out her fantasies of making love to me, as well as her impulse to attack me out of rage that I'm outdoing her academically. But then her superego rises up, and, out of guilt and shame for her same-sex fantasies, she assumes the slayer persona and starts staking people to death. I read about something quite similar in one of Lacan's seminars—"

"DAMMIT! I'M GOING TO LITERALLY BE UP ALL NIGHT RELIVING THIS STUPIDITY. It's not bad enough we've got this *murdered student* here—now we have to listen to your ideas too?"

Parker gasped. She had never been so happy to hear J. Z.'s ranting in her life. But something about Neesa's diatribe nagged at her.

"Just a minute, officers. Neesa, did you just say something about an old French story? What story would that be?"

Neesa rolled her eyes. "Oh, come on, Parker. *Carmilla*, of course. As if you hadn't asked about my thesis a million times."

Officer Sanchez interrupted. "Come on, ladies. This is no time for a fireside chat about literature. We have to get you down to central booking."

"No—wait just one second. Neesa—"

"I don't want to gloat or anything, but I pretty much own that book, and you're clearly obsessed with me."

"*Carmilla*'s not French, you idiot."

"Come on now, young lady," put in an impatient Officer Sanchez. "I'm sure there'll be a copy in the **prison library** . . . "

"*Carmilla*'s not French, you idiot—it's freaking Irish! Even I've figured out that much."

"OK, little lady, that's enough now—"

J. Z. cut in. "Don't you morons understand what she's saying?! Can't you make even the most rudimentary *inferences*? If Neesa doesn't know even the most basic information about her own thesis topic, then that means—work with me here, guys. That's right—you've got it . . . "

"**She didn't write it**," Parker finished for him.

"Shut up, Crowther," barked Neesa. "The murder weapon's in your room. You must have been in on it too. Don't think we don't know you're in love with Parker."

"Ladies, we have a dead body here and a perp in custody. None of this has anything to do with anything." Sanchez was still being as obtuse as ever.

J. Z. rolled his eyes. "Don't you see yet? Who would she have gotten to write it for her but the kid who's obsessed with vampires—Glenn Maxwell? She would have killed him if he threatened to back out and reveal her secret."

"Oh, right, as if that Celtic-studies geek could

prison library: The state pen—not the Harvard Prison, dummy. Although the dank basement of Widener Library might serve just as well . . .

She didn't write it: Submitting work that isn't your own is quite possibly the gravest offense at Harvard. Get caught cheating, copying, or having someone else write your papers for you, and it's the kibosh for you. After undergoing intense interrogations, interviews with military intelligence, and worse—an inquisition from the Ad Board—you'll be booted out for good. Branded a cheater with the big scarlet letter P for Plagiarist on your transcript, you'll never get accepted anywhere else ever again, left to rot in academic hell for all eternity.

handle the complexities of gender theory," said Neesa with a smirk.

"Go look on his computer and see if you don't find the thesis there. Check the document's properties and see if it didn't originate on his machine."

At these words Neesa's face went pale. Suddenly, she turned on her heel, bolted down the stairs, and began sprinting across the Yard—or the closest she could come to sprinting while wearing high-heeled boots, which made it all too easy for the police officers to overtake and apprehend her. Parker, J. Z., and Dunston quickly caught up with them. It was only then that they started to realize what a spectacle they had become. Ever since the police officers crossed the Yard to question Parker, the attention had been completely taken off of poor Glenn and placed squarely on Parker and, now, Neesa Barnett. Students began trickling over from the far sidewalk of Widener to see what the ruckus was about. They had now gathered a few yards away from the brawl. *Crimson* reporter Laura O'Brien was leading the pack, her notebook and pen already being put to (excessive) use.

"What's going on, Laura?" asked Gigi, craning her neck to get a better look. "I can barely hear a thing!"

"The biggest story of the year, that's what," murmured Laura, scribbling furiously. She bit the nib of her pen. "Yes, this will totally beat my story on the ice cream shortage at this year's **Freshman Ice Cream Social."**

Neesa screamed and kicked as Officer Sanchez did his best to hold her down. Her long brown hair spilled messily over her burning eyes, giving her the look of a feral cat.

"Hold still!" barked Officer Nikita.

Officer Sanchez looked around bewilderedly.

"What in God's name is going on?!"

Neesa finally gave up fighting. She fell limp in Officer Sanchez's arms like a little rag doll. With her head hanging, she began to cry. Hot tears streamed down her face, her mascara running in inky streaks.

"You!" she spat out at Parker, "This is all your fault! If you hadn't been there to see Glenn in the pool theater, none of this would've happened."

"One could argue that point," J. Z. said wearily. "But you did murder him, after all."

"Why did you do it, Neesa?" asked Parker. "What was so important that you had to take his life?"

Neesa stared up at her with a dark, hollow stare.

"You don't understand," she hissed. "He was going to go to the dean and confess everything. All my hard work—"

Freshman Ice Cream Social: An awkward Frosh Week mixer at which too little ice cream is served, too many SAT scores are dropped into the conversation, and everyone wishes they were anywhere else. Go anyway.

"You mean his work," interrupted J. Z.

"All I've wanted, all I've worked for during these past four years, was a shot at getting into grad school. And I knew that if I got Glenn to help me, it would be a sure bet. And he seemed perfectly willing—with the right . . . persuasion."

Slut, thought Parker, a little more vindictively than the situation actually called for.

"But he got so wrapped up in it," continued Neesa. "I only needed him to write me something that would earn me a **magna** in the department. My grades were good enough to carry me the rest of the way. But he started treating the thesis like his own child; working obsessively, pulling all-nighters because he just couldn't stop. Telling his friends he was spending the semester abroad was his idea, so he could focus on his research night and day. He was a maniac. Finally, one day in his room, he told me he wasn't going to give me the thesis anymore. He said he wasn't about to share his most brilliant work with someone who not only didn't understand it but didn't appreciate it. He threatened to expose me to the department—to the school—to everyone. I couldn't let him. I worked so hard. I couldn't let him . . . I tried everything to convince him to change his mind—*everything*." Her voice cracked. "So before I left his room, I slipped that jagged broken

magna: Senior theses are awarded grades of *cum laude* (Latin for "with honors"), *magna cum laude* ("with high honors"), and *summa cum laude* ("with the highest honors"). Theses awarded high honors demonstrate unparalleled insight and originality. Getting summa is therefore like getting one of Willy Wonka's golden tickets.

spear shaft into my bag, waited the few days until Intersession, then lured him down to the Adams Pool Theater." She sighed, rubbing her face with her hands. "Before I could move the body out into the snow, I heard Parker's flip-flops. Once she left, I dragged him out and put some snow over him."

"Then you framed me!" exclaimed Parker. "All of that—the attack on you, the stake and the scroll—was all just to freak me out so much that I'd attack you—and get blamed for the murder."

Neesa just looked at the ground silently. Officer Nikita hoisted her up onto her feet. Approaching them from behind was a team of three Cambridge police officers, their **metal badges** glinting in the outdoor lamplight.

metal badges: As opposed to the plastic toy badges favored by the Harvard Police.

"Where is she?" asked one of the officers.

"Right here," said Officer Nikita, handing Neesa over. The officer snapped a pair of metal handcuffs over Neesa's shaking hands.

"Miss Barnett, we're placing you under arrest. You have the right to remain silent—"

"Good luck holding her to that one," said J. Z.

"Anything you say can and will be used against you in a court of law. You have the right to—"

"Wait," said Neesa.

"Yes?"

"Before you take me to the station, can I

please go back to my room to pick up my purse and lip gloss?"

Without another word, the three officers took Neesa away by both arms and slipped into the night, resuming their Miranda reading. The coroner had already arrived on the scene and was making the preparations necessary to transport Glenn's body to the morgue.

Parker gave J. Z. a peck on the check.

"Thank you for believing in me," she said gratefully.

"It wasn't hard," replied J. Z., "plus, you were amazing at solving the mystery. How did you do it?"

"Oh," Parker said coyly, "I have a great coach."

"Did you just lift that line from last week's episode of *Ivory Towers*?" joked J. Z. "I swear the Samantha character was based on you."

Ivory Towers: Harvard's very own online soap opera starring aspiring undergrad actors not talented enough to get cast in anything else.

"Believe me, after all that's happened with Neesa, the only thing I'll be stealing are some warm weather rays on Gibbs Beach."

They walked hand in hand through Johnston Gate and down Mass Ave. With everyone still gathered in Harvard Yard, they were all alone. A crisp, cold gust of wind blew down the street. J. Z. put his arm around Parker and held her tight. Even in the freezing weather, Parker had never felt warmer in her life.

Where It's At

5 Well-Loved Concentrations

Economics

Almost 15 percent of Harvard undergrads concentrate in Ec, making it the most popular concentration. Most will sell their souls to become investment bankers and consultants, go on to business school, become wealthy CEOs, tote that barge, lift that bale, and die lonely, miserable deaths. That's what we impoverished writers like to tell ourselves anyway.

Government

An eclectic mix of over 500 scheming politicos, philosophers, jocks, and others who just didn't know what else to concentrate in, Gov is Harvard's second most popular concentration. Highly respected outside Harvard, reviled within Harvard, Gov is one of the few concentrations you can tailor to your specific interests.

Psych

Beware of these future shrinky-dink shrinks who're always on the lookout for fresh fodder to psychoanalyze. Out of my head!

History

Continually struggling to justify their interest in dead people, History concentrators spend their days digging through archives and their nights writing lengthy papers on past events everyone else has long forgotten. Somehow, though, they maintain an aura of sexiness that the Gov and social studies people just can't muster, no matter how hard they try.

Bio-Chem

These snobby science kids like to think they're soooo much cooler than your average biology or chemistry nerd. And maybe they're right—we've yet to meet a Bio-Chem concentrator we didn't respect.

Epilogue

Officer Sanchez watched them go, his expression placid. Once the Yard was fully deserted, he turned a reproving eye on his partner. "I saw your eyes flash yellow at least four separate times during that interview," he said scornfully.

Officer Nikita hissed. "I couldn't help it—it's that Parker. She's just so . . . delicious looking."

Sanchez cut her off. "How long have you been on the Harvard police force now, Nikita? Seventy years? Seventy-five?" Nikita looked like she was giving it some thought. "How long do you think you're going to last making day-glo eyes in front of a crowd?"

Nikita looked at the ground sullenly, not meeting Sanchez's eyes. Then, after a moment, she asked, "How can we be sure Barnett won't give us up?"

"Don't change the subject. You're not off the hook. But as for Barnett—we're safe there. She'll go to jail, is all. Be back out in fifty years, tops. Not like she'll be any older."

"But what if she turns against us? Or what if she just gets caught—like she almost got caught here?"

"First, she's not dumb enough to turn on us. She knows the master would have her hunted down and destroyed if she put him in any danger. And as for getting caught . . . who's going to catch her in prison? She can kill whoever she wants there, and no one cares. It's like being sent to an all-you-can-eat buffet."

"I'm telling you, Sanchez, I almost bit that Parker woman myself, right there."

Sanchez glanced over at Nikita, menacingly. Slowly, though, the corners of his lips curved into a smile. Finally, he couldn't suppress it any longer and burst out laughing. "Me too! She was some piece, wasn't she? If Barnett could have made that frame stick, I was thinking of paying a late-night visit to Parker in her cell. Now it's going to be a little harder."

"God, you tried everything you could to make it stick— you practically dragged Parker out of there before she could say that she'd figured it out. If that damn J. Z. hadn't shown up . . . But it was Barnett's fault, really. If she had just stopped talking for five minutes, she'd have been home free!"

"She does like to hear herself talk," Sanchez observed. "Still, she sure can think on her feet. I mean, seriously, put yourself in her shoes: Maxwell finds out you're a vampire and comes at you with an improvised stake. But he's too stupid to find your lair, so he comes at you when you're awake! So you just grab his stake and stick it in him. But then someone comes, so you suddenly decide to make Maxwell look like a vampire!

And then you pretend to get attacked, pretend to rise . . . "

"Yeah, she had me bite her," Nikita said, shuddering. "God, drinking vampire blood is creepy."

"It was brilliant, I have to admit. And it almost worked."

The two were silent for a moment.

Finally, Sanchez spoke up. "I'm starving. Let's get a bite to eat."

About the Authors

John Crowther is almost exactly as he is depicted in this story—brilliant, sleepless, and uninterested in your problems unless you are Parker Norcross or someone with something decent to drink. Though he attended Another Ivy League University, he has still managed to eke out a living as a Shakespearean expert. If he had any free time, he would like to spend it deeply drunk on fine wines while hanging around with loose women at the top casinos of the world. Since he doesn't, he mostly reads books about magical creatures and plays video games. He is best known as the editor of the No Fear Shakespeare series but has also made a career of adding vampires to books where they don't belong.

Josh Cracraft ('03) survived three years in Mather without going insane. During his time at Harvard, he befriended teen idols, committed blockcest, dined with gangsters, was spied on by North Korean agents, and changed majors three times.

Unwilling to do anything productive with his life, he intends to become a professor.

Kimberly Holmes ('05) was a staff writer for the Harvard *Lampoon* and sometimes-contributor to *The Harvard Medical Journal* and the magazine *Beer!* She is a current employee of Animation Collective, where she writes cartoon shows for preschoolers and slasher flicks for babies. In her spare time, she enjoys napping, watching TV, and working as a full-time analyst for Goldman Sachs.